THE MYSTERY OF THE VANISHING VIOLINIST

A LADY MILDRED RAMSAY MURDER MYSTERY

RUTH BAKER

CLEANTALES PUBLISHING

Copyright © CleanTales Publishing

First published in November 2025

All characters and events in this publication, other than those clearly in the public domain, are fictitious and any resemblance to real persons, living or dead, is purely coincidental.

Copyright © CleanTales Publishing

The moral right of the author has been asserted.

All rights reserved. This book or any portion thereof may not be reproduced or used in any manner whatsoever without the express written permission of the publisher except for the use of brief quotations in a book review.

For questions and comments about this book, please contact
info@cleantales.com

ISBN: 9798273244283
Imprint: Independently Published

OTHER BOOKS IN THE LADY MILDRED RAMSAY MURDER MYSTERY SERIES

The Mystery of the Disappearing Diamonds
The Mystery of the Final Lap
The Mystery of the Vanishing Violinist
The Mystery of the Christmas Mince Pies

A LADY MILDRED RAMSAY MURDER MYSTERY

BOOK THREE

1

The last rays of a mild autumn evening filtered through the vast glass dome of the Royal Albert Hall, bathing the gathering crowd in a warm amber glow that made even the most modest evening attire shimmer with elegant promise. Lady Mildred Ramsay paused in the entrance foyer, her dark eyes taking in the scene with quiet appreciation. After the wind-swept grittiness of the Brooklands racing circuit during their last adventure and the quiet seclusion of Highfield Manor before that, the grandeur of London's premier concert venue offered shelter from the October chill, a welcome change of scenery.

"Do hurry along, Millie," her brother Henry called from several paces ahead, consulting his pocket watch with a furrowed brow. "We're cutting it terribly fine. The Duke of Hathersfield has reserved seats in his private box, and it simply wouldn't do to arrive after the first movement."

"Heaven forbid we should inconvenience His Grace by being fashionably late," Mildred replied with gentle mockery, though she quickened her pace to appease her brother's sense of propriety. Henry had always been the embodiment of punctuality and protocol, his military bearing testament to years of service. Even now, two years after the Armistice, he carried himself with ramrod straightness, his sandy brown hair neatly parted, his evening attire impeccable.

"It's not merely a matter of inconvenience," Henry insisted, guiding them through the elegant throng towards the grand staircase. "This is a charity concert for war widows and orphans. The Duke chairs the committee, and considering our family's connection to the cause—"

"I'm well aware of the significance, Henry," Mildred cut in, more gently now. Her years as a VAD nurse during the Great War had left her with a profound understanding of such causes. "I merely suggested that arriving three minutes before the programme begins hardly constitutes tardiness."

At that moment, Lady Beatrice Mortimer caught up to them in a whirl of pale blue silk and golden curls, her diminutive figure darting between bemused concert-goers with the agility of a sparrow.

"There you are!" she exclaimed, linking her arm through Mildred's. "I was beginning to think you'd abandoned me to the tender mercies of Lady Ivy Carrington, who's wearing the most absurd turban with feathers that nearly took out poor Mr Sykes's eye when she turned too quickly—you know, that caustic music critic from the Chronicle." She lowered her voice to a theatrical whisper. "And speaking of eyes, have you seen Captain Wilcox in his evening dress? The man looks positively edible."

"Bea," Henry admonished, though his lips twitched with reluctant amusement. "We're at a charitable function, not a matchmaking salon."

"Darling Henry, one can appreciate beauty while supporting a worthy cause," Bea replied with a wink. "Besides, the

Captain has made a tremendous donation. Rumour has it he's pursuing a knighthood."

As they ascended the grand staircase, Mildred observed the vibrant scene of London society in full evening regalia. Ladies in fashionable dropped-waist gowns with glittering beadwork and feathered headbands moved in graceful counterpoint to gentlemen in immaculate black tie. The air thrummed with excited chatter and the lingering scent of expensive perfume.

"The Dowager Countess of Milford has come out of mourning at last," Bea continued, nodding discreetly towards an elderly woman in lavender silk. "Though if you ask me, it's less about the appropriate passage of time and more about Anton Lanyi's performance. They say she hasn't missed one of his concerts since he arrived from Budapest."

"The Hungarian virtuoso has certainly caused quite a stir," Henry remarked as they reached the first-floor landing. "The programme was sold out within hours of being announced."

Mildred nodded, recalling what she had read about the celebrated violinist. Anton Lanyi had emerged from the chaos of post-war Central Europe as a musical sensation, his passionate interpretations of both classical works and his own compositions earning him rapturous reviews across the Continent. His arrival in London had been heralded as the cultural event of the season.

"They say his Guarneri was smuggled out of Hungary during the worst of the troubles," Bea whispered, eyes alight with intrigue. "Wrapped in oilcloth and hidden in a false compartment of a refugee's cart. Can you imagine?"

"I imagine much of what one hears about Maestro Lanyi is carefully cultivated to enhance his mystique," Mildred replied pragmatically. "Though I don't doubt the upheaval in his homeland has shaped his art."

They paused at the entrance to the Duke's private box, where a uniformed attendant checked their invitation cards with stiff formality. As they were ushered inside, Mildred's gaze was drawn to the magnificent auditorium below. Tier upon tier of crimson and gold circled the central space, where the orchestra had begun to assemble on the stage. The enormous pipe organ loomed majestically at the far end, its polished pipes gleaming in the electric light that had long since replaced the original gas illumination.

"How perfectly splendid," Bea murmured, settling into her plush seat. "I do adore the Royal Albert Hall. It's simply the most romantic venue in London."

"I suspect the Prince Consort had more elevated notions than romance when he envisioned it," Henry remarked dryly, arranging the programme notes on his lap with military precision.

"Oh, pish," Bea dismissed with a wave. "Albert was desperately romantic. Why else build such a gloriously extravagant monument to the arts? Besides, just look around —half the affairs in London society begin in these boxes during the interval." She leaned closer to Mildred, nodding towards an adjacent box. "Speaking of which, is that not Mrs Harrington with Colonel Foster? I was quite certain she was meant to be in Bath visiting her ailing mother."

"Bea, really," Mildred admonished, though she couldn't help but follow her friend's gaze. "You've become positively Machiavellian in your interest in other people's indiscretions."

"Not Machiavellian, darling—merely observant. A quality you've taught me to cultivate, I might add." Bea's blue eyes twinkled mischievously. "Though I do wonder what Lady Harrington would say if she knew her husband was escorting the Colonel's wife while she's supposedly nursing her mother through a bout of pleurisy that seems remarkably convenient."

Henry cleared his throat pointedly. "If you two have quite finished dissecting the moral failings of our social circle, the concert is about to begin."

Indeed, the house lights had begun to dim, and a hush fell over the packed auditorium. Mildred settled back in her seat, allowing the atmosphere to wash over her. Despite Bea's frivolity and Henry's stuffiness, she was genuinely looking forward to the evening's performance. Music had always been a refuge for her, especially after the chaos and suffering she had witnessed during the war. There was something about the mathematical precision of classical compositions that soothed her analytical mind while still allowing space for emotion.

As the conductor took his place on the podium to polite applause, Mildred found herself scanning the crowd below. It was a habit she had developed during her nursing days and refined during her unexpected forays into criminal investigation—this quiet observation of human behaviour from a slight remove. She noted Lady Ivy Carrington's strategic positioning near the royal box, the tension in Mrs Sylvia Harcourt's shoulders as she whispered urgently to her companion, the studied boredom of Lord Ravenshaw despite his obvious interest in the young violinist seated in the orchestra's first chair.

The typical games of society, Mildred thought with a small smile. So predictable and yet so endlessly fascinating in their subtle variations. She had never been one for active participation in such theatrics, preferring the role of observer to that of performer. Her natural reticence, combined with her keen eye for detail and logical mind, had served her well both as a nurse and, more recently, as an amateur detective.

The conductor raised his baton, and the first notes of Mozart filled the cavernous space. Bea sighed contentedly, Henry relaxed incrementally, and Mildred allowed herself to be momentarily transported, all thoughts of society intrigue temporarily set aside.

For now, she was simply a woman enjoying beautiful music in a magnificent setting, flanked by her occasionally exasperating but ultimately beloved brother and friend. Tomorrow might bring new puzzles, new challenges, even new dangers—but tonight was for Mozart, for charity, and for the simple pleasure of being alive in a world that, despite its many flaws, still contained such transcendent beauty.

As the music soared and faded beneath the grand dome, Mildred allowed herself to savour the rare sense of calm the evening offered. All around her, London's finest lost themselves in beauty and the comforting rituals of society, unaware of the undercurrents that so often turned even the most glittering occasions unexpectedly dark. For tonight, there was only the promise of music and companionship, but somewhere beyond the candlelit glow, something restless stirred, waiting for its cue. Mildred closed her eyes for a moment of peace, never quite able to shake the feeling—one she'd carried since the war—that serenity in this world was always a fleeting guest.

2

The expectant hush that fell over the Royal Albert Hall deepened as the orchestra completed the opening movement. Mildred noted with amusement how even Bea, usually irrepressible, sat with unusual stillness, her blue eyes wide with anticipation. In the momentary silence between pieces, Mildred caught Henry's glance—he too had been swept up in the music despite his earlier preoccupation with punctuality.

The conductor, Maestro Giulio Moretti, lowered his baton and turned to face the audience. His tall, lean figure cut a dramatic silhouette against the orchestra as he extended one arm with theatrical flourish.

"Ladies and gentlemen," he announced, his Italian accent lending a musical quality to his words, "it is my great honour to present to you the incomparable Maestro Anton Lanyi, performing his own composition, 'Lamentations of Budapest.'"

A wave of enthusiastic applause surged through the hall as a figure emerged from the wings. Anton Lanyi strode onto the stage with the confidence of a man who knew his own worth.

He was not conventionally handsome—his features were too sharp, his dark hair too wild—but he possessed something far more compelling than mere good looks. A crackling energy seemed to emanate from him, an intensity that commanded attention.

"Good heavens," Bea whispered, "he's rather magnificent, isn't he? Like a caged tiger in evening dress."

Henry nodded appreciatively. "They say he survived the revolution by playing for both sides. Remarkable fellow."

Mildred studied the violinist as he bowed to the audience. His formal attire was impeccable, but there was something untamed about him that no tailor could quite disguise. His eyes, deep-set and dark, scanned the audience with a peculiar hunger before settling on his violin.

The instrument itself seemed almost alive in his hands—a gleaming Guarneri with a rich amber varnish that caught the light as he raised it to his chin. For a moment, absolute stillness claimed him. Then, with a nod to Moretti, he drew his bow across the strings.

The first notes were so achingly beautiful that Mildred felt her breath catch. Lanyi played not merely with technical brilliance but with raw emotion that seemed to pour directly from his soul into the instrument. His composition spoke of loss and longing, of a homeland torn by conflict, of beauty discovered amid ruins.

"How extraordinary," Henry murmured, momentarily forgetting his usual reserve. "One can almost see the streets of Budapest."

Indeed, Lanyi's performance transported the audience beyond the gilded walls of the Royal Albert Hall to a world of both tragedy and transcendent beauty. His body swayed with the music, at times seeming to physically wrench the notes from the violin. Sweat beaded on his brow as the piece built to a feverish intensity, then softened to passages of such delicacy that the audience leaned forward collectively, afraid to miss a single note.

Mildred, however, found her attention drawn not only to Lanyi but to the subtle drama unfolding around him. Years of nursing and amateur detection had trained her to notice what others overlooked, and now her gaze wandered to the periphery of the stage.

In the shadows, Moretti conducted with precise, controlled movements that contrasted sharply with the passionate abandon of Lanyi's playing. But beneath the conductor's professional demeanour, Mildred detected tension in the tight set of his shoulders and the occasional flicker of something like resentment when Lanyi embellished a phrase beyond what was written in the score.

At one point, Moretti snapped at a young woman turning pages for the principal cellist, his whispered rebuke sharp enough to make her flinch. The poor girl's cheeks flushed crimson, though she continued her duties with admirable composure.

Mildred's gaze shifted to the first row of the orchestra, where a young violinist—Nora Bellamy, according to the programme—sat clutching her bow with white-knuckled intensity. The girl couldn't be more than twenty, with fair hair pulled severely back and a face that might have been pretty were it not so taut with anxiety. Her eyes never left Lanyi, following his every movement with a mixture of admiration and what looked curiously like fear.

"That girl looks as though she might snap in two," Mildred whispered to Bea. "Seated among the first violins, yet she seems terrified."

"Rumour has it she was to have played a solo tonight," Bea replied, her voice barely audible. "Something changed at the last minute—Sylvia Harcourt's doing, they say."

As if summoned by the mention of her name, Mildred spotted Sylvia Harcourt seated in a box opposite theirs. The widow was known throughout London society as a passionate patron of the arts, particularly where handsome male artists were concerned. Tonight, however, her usual serene elegance was notably absent. She sat rigid in her seat; her face unnaturally pale against her emerald gown, one gloved hand repeatedly touching a pendant at her throat.

"Mrs Harcourt appears rather unwell," Mildred observed. "I wonder what's troubling her."

"Perhaps her chequebook," Bea murmured with characteristic irreverence. "Everyone knows she's been throwing money at Lanyi's concerts like confetti, despite that business with her late husband's investments."

Mildred's attention was drawn back to the stage as Lanyi launched into a particularly challenging passage. The piece had reached its climax, his fingers flying across the strings with supernatural dexterity. Yet even in this moment of artistic triumph, Mildred noticed a man watching from the wings, his stillness a counterpoint to the violinist's kinetic energy.

"Otto Klein," Henry supplied, following her gaze. "Lanyi's accompanist. They've been together since Vienna, I believe."

The man was perhaps in his forties, with the solid build and methodical bearing of someone more comfortable with precision than passion. Unlike the emotional Lanyi, Klein observed the performance with cool detachment, his expression inscrutable. There was something unsettling about his watchfulness, like a chess player calculating moves several plays ahead.

As the piece drew to its conclusion, Lanyi held the final note—a high, tremulous tone that seemed to hover in the air before slowly fading into silence. For a heartbeat, no one moved or breathed. Then the hall erupted in thunderous applause.

Lanyi bowed deeply, his face transformed by a smile that seemed to both invite adoration and maintain distance. Moretti stepped forward to shake his hand, his own smile not quite reaching his eyes. The audience rose to their feet, their enthusiasm building to a crescendo that matched the passion of the performance itself.

"Absolutely extraordinary," Henry declared, applauding vigorously. "Worth every penny of the ticket price, and then some."

Bea dabbed at her eyes with a lace handkerchief. "I shall never forget it. The way he made that violin speak—it was almost supernatural."

Mildred joined in the applause, though her mind was still cataloguing the undercurrents she had observed. "I think I'll stretch my legs during the interval," she said as the applause finally began to subside. "Care to join me?"

"I should love to," Bea replied eagerly. "I've heard the refreshment room has those little almond cakes I adore."

Henry sighed with fond exasperation. "I shall stay here and protect our seats from interlopers. Do try not to get into mischief."

"Us? Mischief? I'm wounded by the very suggestion," Bea protested with mock indignation as she gathered her evening bag and followed Mildred into the corridor.

The interval had transformed the Royal Albert Hall into a bustling hive of conversation and movement. Ladies in evening gowns and gentlemen in formal attire promenaded along the curved corridors, their voices creating a pleasant hum beneath the ornate ceiling. Mildred guided Bea through the crowd with practised ease, ostensibly heading for the refreshment room but subtly steering them towards the passages that led backstage.

"You're not simply looking for almond cakes, are you?" Bea asked, a gleam of excitement in her eyes. "You have that look about you, Millie—the one that means you're puzzling something out."

"I'm merely curious about the dynamics we witnessed," Mildred replied mildly. "There was rather more tension on that stage than the music called for."

They had nearly reached the backstage area when a young man in the uniform of a stagehand hurried past them, his face flushed and anxious. He carried a small wooden box and moved with the frantic energy of someone running late.

"Excuse me," Bea called out, stepping directly into his path with the blithe confidence of a woman used to being accommodated. "Is that for Maestro Lanyi? Might we speak with him? We're terribly impressed with his performance."

The stagehand stopped short, clutching the box to his chest like a shield. He couldn't have been more than twenty, with a shock of sandy hair and a nervous disposition that reminded Mildred of a startled rabbit.

"I—I couldn't say, ma'am," he stammered. "That is, Mr Lanyi doesn't receive visitors during the interval. Strict instructions."

"Oh, how disappointing," Bea pouted prettily. "And here I was hoping to tell him how moved I was by his

'Lamentations.' The section representing the uprising was positively revolutionary."

The young man shifted uncomfortably. "It's not my place to say, ma'am, but there'll be fireworks tonight, and no mistake." He glanced over his shoulder, then leaned closer, lowering his voice. "Between the maestro and Moretti and that Mrs Harcourt—it's like a powder keg back there. If you'll excuse me, I need to deliver this rosin before I lose my position."

He darted away before either of them could respond, disappearing through a door marked "Authorised Personnel Only."

"Well!" Bea exclaimed. "That was intriguing. Fireworks, indeed! What do you suppose he meant?"

"I'm not entirely sure," Mildred replied thoughtfully, "but I suspect we're witnessing more than one performance tonight."

A commotion from beyond the door caught their attention—raised voices, one with Moretti's distinctive Italian inflection, followed by the sound of something being knocked over. Then silence, more ominous than the outburst that preceded it.

"Perhaps we should return to our seats," Mildred suggested, though her expression remained thoughtful. "The second half will begin shortly."

As they made their way back through the crowded corridor, Bea chattered happily about the prospect of more almond cakes, but Mildred's mind was elsewhere. The young stagehand's words echoed in her thoughts, along with the moments of tension she had observed. Moretti's frustration, Nora's anxiety, Sylvia's unease, Klein's watchfulness—each seemed a separate thread in a complex tapestry whose pattern she couldn't yet discern.

What had the stagehand meant by *fireworks*? A mere metaphor for artistic temperaments, or something more specific? And why had he seemed so nervous—beyond the ordinary anxiety of service staff in the presence of their social betters?

As they returned to the Duke's box, Henry greeted them with raised eyebrows. "I trust you found refreshment? The lights will dim momentarily."

"Indeed," Mildred replied, settling into her seat. "Though I suspect the second half may prove even more interesting than the first."

The lights began to fade, signalling the end of the interval. As the audience quieted in anticipation, Mildred couldn't shake the feeling that beneath the glitter and beauty of the evening, something dark and discordant was building toward an unexpected crescendo. The stagehand's nervous prediction of "fireworks" had lodged in her mind like a splinter.

The stage was reset, the orchestra reassembled, and Maestro Moretti emerged once more to enthusiastic applause. As he raised his baton, Mildred found herself watching not for Anton Lanyi's entrance, but for the subtle interactions that would reveal the true composition being played tonight—one of human ambition, jealousy, and fear, performed in the shadows behind the music.

3

Mozart's violin concerto unfurled through the hall, its melancholy eloquence drawing the audience forward in one breath. Lanyi stood in the spotlight, bow sure and singing, the air sharpened by that shimmering hush which falls when great music finds its mark.

Mildred leaned forward in her seat, captivated despite herself. There was something almost supernatural about the way Lanyi commanded not only his violin but the very atmosphere of the hall. His eyes were closed in concentration, his dark hair falling across his forehead as he reached the climax of the movement.

"He's rather magnificent, isn't he?" whispered Beatrice beside her. "Even Henry looks impressed, and you know how he feels about these continental types."

Indeed, Henry sat with unusual stillness, his opera glasses trained on the stage. Mildred smiled to herself. Her brother rarely admitted to enjoying anything that wasn't thoroughly British in origin.

The concerto was building towards its most stirring passage when something changed. At first, it was barely perceptible—a slight hesitation, a fractionally missed note. Mildred tilted her head, listening more intently. Something was wrong. The virtuoso's rhythm faltered, his bow trembling across the strings.

Anton's eyes flew open. He stared out into the audience with such a profound expression of confusion that a murmur rippled through the hall. His left hand dropped from the fingerboard, the violin dangling precariously from his grip.

"What on earth is he playing at?" Henry muttered, lowering his opera glasses.

Mildred didn't answer. She was watching as the musician's face contorted in what appeared to be pain. He took a faltering step forward, his bow clattering to the polished floor. The conductor turned, his baton suspended in mid-air, as the orchestra stumbled into uncertain silence.

Then, with terrible finality, Anton Lanyi crumpled to the stage, his precious violin hitting the floorboards with a discordant twang that seemed to echo in the stunned silence.

For one heartbeat, nobody moved. Then pandemonium erupted.

"Good heavens!" Bea clutched Mildred's arm, her face pale. "I didn't expect such theatrics in the middle of Mozart!"

All around them, the audience was rising to its feet. Ladies gasped behind gloved hands, gentlemen called out for doctors, and the orchestra members abandoned their instruments, clustering at the edge of the stage.

Maestro Moretti was kneeling beside the fallen violinist, frantically loosening his collar. "Stand back!" he shouted, his Italian accent thickening with distress. "Give him air!"

Mildred rose from her seat. "We should help," she said quietly to Henry and Bea. Her nursing experience during the war had taught her to remain calm in crises.

Henry hesitated, then nodded, following Mildred as she made her way towards the stage. Bea trailed behind them, fumbling in her reticule for her smelling salts. "Just in case," she murmured, though whether for Anton or herself remained unclear.

By the time they reached the stage, a distinguished-looking gentleman with a medical bag was already bending over the violinist, his fingers pressed against Anton's neck. A hush fell over the nearby crowd as the doctor straightened up, his expression grave.

"I'm afraid there's nothing to be done," he announced. "The gentleman is dead."

A collective gasp swept through the hall. Bea swayed dramatically, her knees buckling. "Oh, my goodness," she breathed, fumbling with her smelling salts. "I may need to sit down."

Henry steadied her with a firm hand on her elbow. "Pull yourself together, Beatrice," he murmured, though his own face had gone rather grey.

Mildred stepped closer to the stage, watching as Moretti crossed himself, his dark eyes wide with shock. Behind him, she could see Nora Bellamy, the young understudy violinist, her hands pressed to her mouth in horror. Otto Klein, the accompanist, stood to one side, his face an expressionless mask that nonetheless seemed to convey deep distress.

"Such a tragedy," murmured a woman in an elaborate feathered hat to Mildred's right. "He seemed perfectly well just moments ago."

"It must have been his heart," suggested her companion.

But a thin man in spectacles shook his head. "Did you see his face? The way he clutched at his throat? I've seen such symptoms before..."

"What are you suggesting?" the feathered lady demanded.

The man lowered his voice, though not enough to prevent Mildred from hearing his next words: "Poison, madam. The poor fellow was poisoned."

The whisper spread through the crowd like wildfire. "Poison?" "Did he say poison?" "How dreadful!" "Who would do such a thing?"

Sylvia Harcourt, Anton's wealthy patroness, pushed her way through the throng, her face ashen beneath her elegant makeup. "This is absurd," she declared. "Anton was in perfect health. There must be some mistake."

Mildred observed her closely. Was that genuine distress in her voice, or merely the fear of scandal? The woman's gloved hands twisted nervously at her pearl necklace.

On stage, the doctor was conducting a cursory examination. "I cannot determine the cause of death without a proper post-mortem," he announced, "but I cannot rule out the possibility of... unnatural causes."

This pronouncement sent fresh ripples of excitement and horror through the crowd. Bea, who had recovered somewhat from her near-swoon, leaned close to Mildred. "Well, this is becoming more interesting by the minute. Though rather ghastly, of course," she added hastily.

Henry huffed. "The police will need to be called. This is most irregular."

"They're already on their way," said a stagehand who had materialised at Henry's elbow. "The manager telephoned Scotland Yard straight away."

Mildred nodded absently, her attention caught by something near the fallen violinist. A small dark-glass apothecary bottle had rolled from Anton's pocket and now lay beside his outstretched hand. No one else appeared to have noticed it yet.

Without drawing attention to herself, she moved a little closer to the stage, straining to read the label on the bottle. It appeared to be some sort of tonic, perhaps for nerves before performances. But if the whispers of poison were true...

"Look at his violin," Bea whispered, nudging Mildred gently. "It doesn't seem to be damaged, despite the fall."

Indeed, the instrument lay on its side, remarkably intact. As Mildred watched, Arthur Pike, the stage manager, carefully picked it up and placed it in its open case, which sat on a nearby chair.

"Careful with that," snapped Moretti. "It's worth more than this entire concert."

Pike nodded nervously; the heavy ring of brass keys at his belt gave a muted jangle as he hovered, then left the lid unlatched for logging. As he did so, Mildred noticed a peculiar detail—a small scratch near the lock of the case, fresh and bright against the polished wood.

Before she could ponder its significance, the rear doors of the hall swung open, and a tall figure in a dark suit strode purposefully down the central aisle.

"That must be the detective," Bea murmured. "Rather handsome, in a severe sort of way."

Mildred watched as the newcomer, who looked vaguely familiar, surveyed the scene with sharp eyes. "Yes," she agreed quietly. "And I have a feeling this evening is about to become even more complicated than we imagined."

She glanced once more at Anton's body, now being discreetly covered with a velvet stage curtain. What had caused the virtuoso to collapse so suddenly, in the middle of his greatest performance? Was it truly poison, as the whispers suggested? And if so, who among the assembled musicians, patrons, and admirers had wished him harm?

The detective was now speaking to the hall manager, his notebook already in hand. Soon, Mildred knew, he would begin questioning witnesses—and they would all find themselves caught in the opening movements of a very different kind of composition: a symphony of secrets, lies, and perhaps murder.

4

The velvet curtain lay across Anton Lanyi's still form, casting an eerie shadow on the polished stage floor. The hall's magnificent chandeliers, which had earlier bathed the audience in golden light, now seemed harsh and intrusive, illuminating shock on every face. The orchestra members stood in bewildered clusters, instruments forgotten in their hands, while ushers attempted vainly to guide patrons back to their seats.

Mildred observed it all with the detached clarity that had served her well during her nursing days. Beside her, Beatrice dabbed at her eyes with a lace handkerchief, while Henry maintained a protective hand on his sister's elbow.

"Who is that?" Bea whispered, nodding toward the tall man striding down the centre aisle.

Mildred watched as he approached, noting his purposeful gait and the sharp intelligence in his grey eyes. A smile of recognition touched her lips. "Inspector Kent. It seems Scotland Yard has been summoned with impressive haste."

"Oh, your inspector has arrived!" Bea brightened considerably despite the grim circumstances. "How fortunate that we're present for another investigation."

"He's hardly 'my' inspector," Mildred corrected, though she couldn't suppress a small smile. "Though I daresay he'll be surprised to find us here."

Henry sighed heavily. "Not another murder, Millie. We've barely recovered from that business at Brooklands with the sabotaged racing car."

"And before that, the disappearing diamonds at Highfield Manor," Bea added with inappropriate enthusiasm. "We do seem to encounter an unusual number of suspicious deaths."

Inspector Charles Kent paused briefly to speak with the hall manager before making his way to the stage. Up close, Mildred could see that the past months had added a new line or two around his eyes, but his gaze was as keen as ever—pale blue, analytical, missing nothing.

That gaze swept the room, pausing briefly on each face before settling, with evident surprise, on Mildred and her companions.

"Lady Mildred," he said, a complex mix of emotions colouring his voice—professional respect, personal wariness, and perhaps a hint of something warmer. "I hadn't expected to find you involved in another suspicious death."

"Nor I you, Inspector Kent," she replied evenly, unconsciously touching the small notepad in her pocket. "Though I suppose it was inevitable our paths would cross again given our respective pursuits."

"Inevitable?" A hint of a smile touched his lips. "Because crime follows me, or because trouble follows you?"

"I prefer to think we're both simply drawn to puzzles that need solving."

Kent nodded to Henry and Bea. "Lord Ramsay, Lady Beatrice. I trust you've been well since our adventure at Brooklands."

"Splendidly so, Inspector," Bea replied brightly. "Though I still can't look at a racing car without checking for sabotage."

Henry merely nodded, his military bearing as precise as ever. "Inspector. I suppose you'll be wanting statements from everyone. A rather large undertaking in a concert hall."

"Indeed, Lord Ramsay. Though I'll prioritise those closest to the victim." Kent turned his attention back to Mildred. "Were you acquainted with Mr Lanyi?"

"Not personally," Mildred replied. "We were simply attending the concert. Though I observed him closely during his performance, of course."

"Of course," Kent agreed, with a hint of dryness in his tone. "And did you notice anything unusual before his collapse?"

"He seemed in perfect form initially," Mildred said thoughtfully. "But then he faltered—touched his throat, looked confused. Within moments, he had collapsed."

Kent made a note in his small leather-bound notebook. "Consistent with other accounts. Would you mind providing a more detailed statement while my men speak with the orchestra members?"

"By all means," she replied, ignoring Henry's disapproving frown.

Kent gestured toward a quiet corner near the stage. As they walked, Mildred noticed Maestro Moretti gesticulating wildly to a constable, his face flushed with emotion.

"Your conductor seems rather upset," she observed.

Kent glanced over. "Indeed. Though that may simply be an artistic temperament, as some have suggested."

"Or genuine shock," Mildred countered. "Not everyone expresses grief in stoic English fashion, Inspector."

"A fair point, Lady Mildred. You seem remarkably composed yourself."

"I've seen death before, Inspector. Though never quite so dramatically staged."

"Most people haven't witnessed a man being poisoned during a violin concerto."

"So you're certain it was poison?"

"I'm certain of nothing yet, Lady Mildred. That's why I'm conducting an investigation rather than making pronouncements."

"A refreshing approach," she replied with the ghost of a smile. "Too many people leap to conclusions."

"Like the whispers of poison already circulating among your fellow audience members?" There was a dry humour in his voice that surprised her.

"Precisely. Though I will admit the symptoms were... suggestive."

They had reached a quiet alcove where Kent indicated she should sit. Taking out his notebook, he began to question her methodically about the evening's events, the concert, and her observations of Anton's collapse. Mildred answered concisely, appreciating his precise, untheatrical approach.

"And did you notice anything unusual before the performance?" Kent asked. "Any interactions that seemed tense or out of place?"

Mildred considered. "Maestro Moretti was particularly sharp with a page-turner. Mrs Harcourt appeared agitated even before the performance began. And the young violinist—"

"Nora Bellamy," Kent supplied.

"Yes. She seemed extremely nervous, beyond what one might expect of an understudy."

Kent made careful notes. "You have an eye for human behaviour, Lady Mildred."

"People reveal themselves in small ways, Inspector. I find it... interesting."

"A diplomatic word for 'telling'," he remarked, the corner of his mouth twitching. "Now, if you wouldn't mind waiting while I speak with the musicians, I may have additional questions."

As Kent moved away to begin questioning the orchestra members, Bea hurried over, her eyes bright with curiosity.

"What did the inspector want?" she asked, settling beside Mildred.

"My observations of the evening. And he's doing his job, Bea, not auditioning for a novel."

"Still, you must admit he has a certain brooding quality. It's clear he's pleased to see you again, despite his professional demeanour."

"I doubt Inspector Kent would appreciate the comparison," Mildred replied with a small smile. "And our previous investigations at Highfield and Brooklands were purely professional collaborations."

"If you say so, darling," Bea replied with a knowing look. "Though I didn't imagine the warmth in his eyes when he spotted you."

Henry joined them, his expression stern. "I hope you're not planning to involve yourself in this investigation, Millie. Twice is coincidence, but three times begins to look like a habit."

"I have no intention of involving myself, Henry," Mildred assured him, though the notepad in her pocket suggested otherwise. "I'm merely providing the Inspector with my observations, as any responsible witness would."

They watched as Kent methodically interviewed each musician, his manner professional but probing. When he spoke with Moretti, the conductor's voice rose several times, his hands slicing the air emphatically.

"...impossible demands! The man was brilliant but impossible. He insisted on changing tempos without warning, argued over every interpretation!"

Kent remained impassive. "And these disagreements, they were professional only?"

"What are you suggesting?" Moretti bristled.

"I'm gathering information, Maestro, not making accusations."

Mildred's attention shifted to where Sylvia Harcourt sat whispering urgently with a thin man in pinstripes. She caught fragments: "...the contract clearly states..." and "...if there's an investigation into finances..."

Interesting, Mildred thought. Patronage often came with financial entanglements, but Sylvia's distress seemed extreme.

Nora Bellamy was next to be questioned, twisting a handkerchief between her fingers as she spoke. The young violinist kept glancing at Anton's covered form, her face pale with shock.

"...completely devastated. He was my mentor, my inspiration..."

"Yet you were his understudy," Kent observed. "Did that create tension?"

"Of course not! I was honoured to learn from him."

Kent made a note. "And your relationship was strictly professional?"

Nora's cheeks flushed. "I don't appreciate what you're implying, Inspector."

Otto Klein, the accompanist, maintained an unsettling calm throughout his interview. His face remained expressionless; his answers were brief and precise. Only his fingers, tapping softly against his thigh in what Mildred recognised as a pianist's habit, betrayed any inner agitation.

While Kent continued his questioning, Mildred rose and wandered closer to the stage, ostensibly admiring the architecture of the great hall. From this vantage point, she could see the small brown bottle she had noticed earlier, now half-hidden beneath the edge of the curtain covering Anton.

With a quick glance to ensure no one was watching, she knelt to examine it more closely. The label was partially obscured, but she could make out "Tonic" and what appeared to be a Hungarian pharmacy mark. The cork lay nearby, as if it had been recently opened.

Careful not to touch anything, Mildred shifted slightly to examine Anton's violin case, which still sat on the chair where Arthur Pike had placed it. The scratch she had noticed earlier was definitely fresh—a bright line against the polished wood near the lock. Leaning closer, she observed that the scratch wasn't random; it appeared to follow the edge of what might be a concealed panel.

"Finding clues, Lady Mildred?"

She straightened to find Inspector Kent regarding her with a mixture of irritation and amusement.

"Merely satisfying my curiosity, Inspector," she replied evenly. "Though you might want to examine that tonic bottle before someone inadvertently kicks it under the stage."

"I appreciate your concern for the evidence, but I would prefer you leave the investigating to Scotland Yard."

"Naturally. I wouldn't dream of interfering."

His expression suggested he didn't entirely believe her. "The bottle has been noted, as has the violin case. Both will be examined thoroughly."

"I'm glad to hear it. The case is particularly interesting, don't you think? That scratch seems quite fresh."

Kent studied her for a moment. "You notice a great deal for someone with no connection to this affair."

"As I mentioned, it's a habit," she replied with a small smile. "A habit that served us well at both Highfield Manor and Brooklands, if you recall."

"Indeed it did," Kent conceded with unexpected frankness. "Your insights proved invaluable in both cases, despite my initial resistance."

"Are you actually admitting that my 'amateur interference' was helpful, Inspector?" Mildred asked, recalling his earlier criticisms during their first case together.

"I believe in acknowledging facts, Lady Mildred," Kent replied with the hint of a smile. "And the fact is, your observations have a way of illuminating paths others might miss."

Their eyes met in a moment of mutual understanding, professional respect tinged with something more complex. Mildred was the first to look away, glancing toward where Bea was attempting to comfort a distraught usherette.

"I should collect my companions, Inspector. Unless you need us further?"

"Not at present. Though I would ask that you remain available for additional questions." He handed her a card. "My office details, should you recall anything else of significance."

Mildred tucked the card into her reticule. "I shall keep it at hand."

As she turned to leave, Kent added, "One final question, Lady Mildred. What makes you so certain this was murder?"

She paused, considering her answer carefully. "I never said it was, Inspector. But a man of Anton Lanyi's reputation doesn't simply collapse during his greatest performance without reason. And reasons have a way of leading to people."

"Indeed they do," Kent agreed solemnly. "Good evening, Lady Mildred."

As she collected Bea and Henry and made their way toward the exit, Mildred couldn't help glancing back at the stage. In the harsh electric light, Anton's covered form seemed smaller somehow, diminished by death. Yet the mystery surrounding him had already begun to grow, expanding to encompass everyone in that gilded hall.

Who among them had silenced the virtuoso's music forever? And what secrets lay hidden in that scratched violin case, waiting to be discovered?

5

The morning after Anton Lanyi's tragic collapse brought a sharp chill to the London air. Mist hung over the streets, shrouding carriages and motorcars in ghostly veils as Lady Mildred Ramsay made her way towards Scotland Yard. She had telephoned ahead to Inspector Kent, citing "additional observations" she felt compelled to share.

In truth, she had spent half the night poring over the details she had committed to her small notebook—the peculiar scratch on Anton's violin case, the overturned tonic bottle with its Hungarian pharmacy mark, the varied expressions of shock and perhaps calculation on the faces of those nearest the stage. Sleep had eluded her, and breakfast had been a perfunctory affair of toast and strong tea.

"You're becoming obsessed," Henry had remarked over the morning paper, eyebrows raised in disapproval. "This is the third time you've entangled yourself in police matters. People will talk."

"Let them," Mildred had replied with a small smile. "It's far more interesting than being talked about for my hats or my prospects for marriage."

Now, as she approached the imposing stone building, she rehearsed what she would say to Kent. Their previous encounters had taught her that he respected precision and disliked dramatisation. She would need to present her concerns about the violin case as observations, not theories—at least initially.

The inspector was waiting in a small, austere office, a stack of preliminary reports before him. He rose when Mildred entered, offering a brisk nod that nonetheless carried a hint of warmth.

"Lady Mildred. Punctual as ever."

"Inspector Kent. Buried in paperwork as ever."

A ghost of a smile touched his lips. "You mentioned additional observations in your telephone call. I trust they're more substantive than society gossip about Anton's admirers?"

"Far more concrete," Mildred replied, settling into the wooden chair he offered. "I've been thinking about that violin case."

Kent's expression shifted subtly—interest mingled with wariness. "The one you were examining without permission?"

"The very same," she agreed, unruffled by his gentle admonishment. "Has it been thoroughly searched?"

"Of course. Standard procedure."

"And did your officers notice anything unusual about its construction?"

Kent hesitated, his gaze sharpening. "Such as?"

"Such as the possibility of a false bottom or hidden

compartment. The scratch I noticed appeared to follow a line inconsistent with the case's visible structure."

For a moment, Kent considered her words, tapping his pencil against the edge of his desk. "The case was examined and catalogued along with Mr Lanyi's other effects. Nothing extraordinary was noted."

Mildred felt a familiar stir of frustration. "Might I see it? I have a particular interest in craftsmanship."

"I wasn't aware you were a connoisseur of violin cases, Lady Mildred."

"I'm a connoisseur of curiosities, Inspector. And that case struck me as curious indeed."

After a brief internal debate visible in the slight furrow of his brow, Kent rose. "Very well. The evidence is being held in the secure room. Follow me."

They walked in companionable silence through the stone corridors of Scotland Yard, past bustling officers and the occasional handcuffed suspect. Mildred was reminded of hospital corridors during the war—the same purposeful atmosphere, the same undercurrent of gravity beneath routine tasks.

The evidence room was a stark, windowless chamber with shelves of labelled boxes and a long table in the centre. A constable sat at a small desk, maintaining the log of items entering and leaving police custody.

"The violin case from the Royal Albert Hall incident, please, Parsons," Kent requested.

The constable retrieved a familiar leather case, placing it carefully on the central table. "Here you are, sir. Though I should mention, it's been officially requested for inspection by the insurance adjuster later today. Mrs Harcourt has filed a claim."

"Has she indeed?" Mildred murmured, exchanging a look with Kent.

"Noted," Kent replied. "We'll be brief."

When the constable had returned to his desk, Kent gestured for Mildred to examine the case. "What exactly are you looking for?"

Rather than answering directly, Mildred ran her gloved fingers lightly over the surface, tracing the scratch she had noticed the previous night. It was indeed precisely where she remembered, cutting across the polished leather near the lock mechanism.

"Do you mind if I...?" she asked, gesturing toward the lock.

Kent hesitated, then nodded. "Carefully. This is evidence, not a museum piece."

Mildred opened the case, revealing the velvet-lined interior shaped to cradle Anton's precious violin. The instrument itself was notably absent.

"The violin is being assessed separately," Kent explained, seeing her questioning look. "Its value requires special handling."

Mildred nodded absently, her attention focused on the interior of the case. She ran her fingers along the edges, pressed gently against the velvet lining, tapped lightly against the sides. Then, with greater deliberation, she tapped along the bottom of the case, moving systematically from one end to the other.

In the hush of the room, the difference stood out. The case gave the steady thump of wood beneath its padding—except for one side, where the sound turned hollow, faint but impossible to ignore.

"Did you hear that?" she asked, tapping again to demonstrate.

Kent leaned closer, his shoulder nearly touching hers as he listened. "It does sound... different."

"Hollow," Mildred said firmly, tapping once more. "This section doesn't match the rest. The depth doesn't correspond to the exterior dimensions."

"Suggesting?"

"A hidden compartment, Inspector. One accessed, I suspect, from this area near the lock."

She traced the scratch again, applying gentle pressure with her fingertips. Nothing moved.

"If there is a mechanism, it's not obvious," she admitted, frowning slightly.

"Or perhaps it's simply the construction method," Kent countered. "Violin cases aren't built like ordinary boxes. The acoustics alone require special consideration."

Mildred pursed her lips. "True, but that doesn't explain the scratch. It's fresh, Inspector—newer than the case itself. Someone attempted to access something here, and recently."

"Pure conjecture, Lady Mildred."

"Informed observation," she corrected mildly. "Based on evidence you can hear for yourself."

To demonstrate her point, she tapped a solid section, then the hollow one. Kent's expression remained sceptical, but he bent closer to listen. In doing so, his hand brushed accidentally against the side of the case near the lock—and there was a soft, almost imperceptible click.

They both froze, eyes meeting in surprised recognition.

"Did you—?" Mildred began.

"I heard it," Kent confirmed, his professional reserve momentarily forgotten.

With careful movements, he pressed the area again, and this time a small panel beside the lock eased open, revealing a narrow space between the outer case and the inner lining.

"Well, I'll be damned," Kent murmured, then immediately looked embarrassed at his lapse into profanity. "Pardon my language."

"I believe the situation warrants it," Mildred replied, unable to suppress a small smile of triumph. "Shall we see what our virtuoso was hiding?"

Kent reached carefully into the newly revealed space, his fingers exploring the hidden compartment. After a moment, he withdrew his hand with a frown. "It's empty."

"Empty?" Mildred echoed, disappointment evident in her voice. "Are you certain?"

"See for yourself," he offered, stepping back slightly.

Mildred peered into the space, confirming Kent's assessment. The compartment was indeed empty, though she noted faint impressions in the velvet lining, suggesting something had once rested there.

"Whatever it contained is gone," she said, straightening. "Taken before the case came into police custody, I presume."

"Or there was nothing to begin with," Kent suggested. "It

could have been used for spare strings, rosin, a polishing cloth—any number of innocent items."

"In a secret compartment activated by a hidden mechanism?" Mildred's eyebrow arched sceptically. "That seems rather elaborate for rosin, Inspector."

The telephone in the evidence room rang, startling them both. The constable answered, then held the receiver toward Kent. "For you, sir. The coroner's office with preliminary findings."

As Kent took the call, Mildred continued her examination of the case, running her fingers along the interior of the hidden compartment. The velvet lining was slightly worn in places, suggesting frequent use. Whatever had been concealed here had been removed and replaced many times.

"You were right," Kent said when he returned, his expression grave. "The coroner confirms traces of cyanide. Anton Lanyi was poisoned."

Mildred nodded, unsurprised. "The symptoms were consistent. Did they determine how it was administered?"

"Preliminary findings suggest it was in something he ingested shortly before his performance. Possibly—"

"The tonic," Mildred finished. "I noticed a small brown bottle near his body. If potassium cyanide was present and he took it just before going on stage—"

"It would explain the timing of his collapse," Kent agreed. "We're having the bottle tested now."

They lapsed into thoughtful silence, both contemplating the implications of their discoveries.

"This case has become considerably more complicated," Kent finally said, gesturing toward the violin case. "A secret compartment, a poisoned tonic... it suggests premeditation and, possibly, a motive beyond personal animosity."

"I had a thought about that," Mildred said carefully. "During the war, there were rumours about musicians transporting valuables across borders—jewels, documents, currency. Items small enough to conceal in instrument cases but valuable enough to warrant the risk."

"Smuggling?" Kent's eyebrows rose. "That's quite a leap from a hidden compartment to international intrigue, Lady Mildred."

"Is it? Anton was Hungarian and fled after the war. Europe is still in turmoil, with borders redrawn, fortunes lost and desperate to be recovered. A celebrated violinist travels freely between countries, above suspicion..."

Kent's expression remained dubious. "It sounds like something from one of your detective novels."

"Truth is often stranger than fiction, Inspector."

"Perhaps. But I prefer to begin with the obvious motives before speculating about smuggling rings. Jealousy, ambition, money—these are the usual suspects in murder cases."

Mildred felt a familiar flush of irritation. "And the hidden compartment? How does that fit your 'obvious motives' theory?"

"It could relate to any number of private matters—love letters, gambling debts, personal secrets. Not everything is an international conspiracy, Lady Mildred."

Before she could reply, they were interrupted by a light tap at the door. Beatrice's bright face appeared, her hat at a slightly askew angle that suggested she had hurried.

"There you are, Mildred! I've been looking everywhere. Henry said you'd gone to Scotland Yard, and I simply had to come along. Have I missed anything thrilling?"

Kent suppressed a sigh as Bea swept into the room, her gaze immediately fixing on the open violin case.

"Oh! Are we examining clues? How perfectly detective-like!"

"Lady Beatrice," Kent acknowledged with a polite nod that didn't quite mask his resigned expression. "Lady Mildred was just sharing her... theories."

"Observations," Mildred corrected. "Based on evidence. We've discovered a hidden compartment in Anton's violin case, Bea. Empty now, but clearly designed for secrecy."

Bea's eyes widened with delight. "A secret compartment? How thrilling! What do you suppose he kept in it? Love letters from adoring fans? Sheet music stolen from rivals? Perhaps sandwiches for those long performances?"

Despite her frustration with Kent, Mildred couldn't help smiling at Bea's irrepressible humour. "I doubt Mr Lanyi hid refreshments in his violin case. But during the war, there were stories about musicians smuggling valuables across borders—jewels, documents, currency."

"Jewels! Oh, how dramatic," Bea exclaimed. "Though I suppose one would need sandwiches too, for a proper smuggling expedition. Crime is hungry work."

Kent cleared his throat. "As I was explaining to Lady Mildred, while the compartment is certainly curious, leaping to conclusions about smuggling rings is premature. We'll investigate all possibilities, of course."

The dismissive note in his voice rekindled Mildred's irritation. "Of course," she agreed, her tone cooling. "Far be it from me to suggest anything beyond the commonplace."

Kent caught her tone, his gaze meeting hers with a hint of challenge. "I'm simply advocating for methodical investigation over speculation, Lady Mildred. A principle I believe you've appreciated in our previous... collaborations."

"When the evidence points clearly in one direction, Inspector, it's not speculation to follow it."

An unspoken tension hummed between them, the remnants of old disagreements about intuition versus procedure that had marked their previous cases together.

Bea glanced between them, astute enough to sense the undercurrents. "Well! While you two debate methodology, shall I examine this marvellous case more closely? Perhaps I'll discover a second compartment with actual sandwiches."

Her deliberate lightness broke the tension. Kent stepped back with a small nod, allowing her access to the table.

"By all means, Lady Beatrice. Though I must ask you not to touch anything without gloves."

As Bea donned the proffered gloves and bent over the case with exaggerated care, Mildred moved slightly aside, her thoughts racing. Kent's dismissal of her theory stung more than she cared to admit. After their previous cases together, she had hoped he might give her insights more credence.

Yet his scepticism only strengthened her resolve. If Anton Lanyi had been involved in smuggling valuables, and if that involvement had somehow led to his murder, the truth would emerge—with or without Inspector Kent's initial support.

As Kent moved to speak with the constable about the insurance adjuster's upcoming visit, Mildred made a silent promise to herself. She would follow her instincts, pursue her own inquiries, and discover what Anton had been hiding in that hollow space—and why someone had been desperate enough to silence him forever.

Beside her, Bea tapped experimentally on the case, mimicking Mildred's earlier actions. "It really does sound hollow, doesn't it?" she murmured. "Like there's a whole other world inside."

"Yes," Mildred agreed quietly, watching Kent's back as he stood in conversation across the room. "And I intend to discover exactly what that world contained—no matter who dismisses the possibility."

The gleam in her eye would have been instantly recognisable to anyone who knew her well—the spark that ignited whenever a puzzle presented itself, demanding to be solved. It was the same look she had worn at Highfield Manor and Brooklands, in the moments before she began unravelling murders that others deemed impenetrable.

Anton Lanyi's secrets would be no different. Whether they hid in hollow violin cases or coded sheet music, she would bring them into the light—if only to prove to a certain sceptical inspector that her intuition was worth heeding.

6

The sky above Kensington was pewter grey as Mildred strode briskly from Scotland Yard. Frustration warred with anticipation; Inspector Kent's almost wilful dismissal of the clues she had uncovered gnawed at her. Had she truly expected him to leap into the arms of speculation? Hardly – but after all their cases together, his stubborn adherence to procedure was beginning to chafe.

Still, her instincts, honed through more than just idle society gossip, prickled with the sense that something had not yet revealed itself about Anton Lanyi's mysterious end. She'd always trusted those instincts, even when others didn't.

She was halfway down Exhibition Road, deep in thought, when she abruptly remembered the childish habit she'd cultivated during the war: to retrace every step when a mystery confounded her. As she reached the corner, she turned about and walked straight back to the Royal Albert Hall, the scene of that fateful concert. The constables now set to guard the place recognised her name and waved her through with murmured respect; Mildred gave no cause for them to regret it.

Inside, the once-vivid echoes of applause and gasps had faded, replaced by the shallow emptiness left in the wake of murder. She surveyed the deserted musicians' dressing area, eyes searching for anything missed in the previous night's tumult.

It was Bea who found her ten minutes later, tottering across the corridor in a pair of shoes far more suited to salons than sleuthing.

"There you are!" Bea exclaimed with mock exasperation, cheeks flushed. "Henry nearly had a fit when he realised both of us had vanished at breakfast. He's convinced we'll be next to collapse in public."

Mildred suppressed a smile. "Did you come to bolster my resolve or sabotage my investigation with cake crumbs?"

"Oh, both," Bea replied cheerfully, producing a slightly battered packet of lemon creams. "But really, Millie, what do you expect to find here? The scene's already been so thoroughly trampled by detectives and gossips and insurance men it's a wonder there's a single clue left."

Sometimes, though, clues endured where memory and logic failed. As they approached the vacant dressing room assigned to Anton, Mildred's attention snagged on a shred of paper near the leg of a battered piano stool. It was nearly camouflaged by scuff marks and the odd stray feather from a well-worn boa. While Bea amused herself with the locks on the old trunk by the window, Mildred knelt and retrieved the scrap, smoothing it out against her skirts.

A chill ran through her. The paper was unmistakably torn from a page of violin sheet music, but the notes scrawled upon it meandered drunkenly, out of rhythm, slashing the staves at foreign angles. Crowded between the bars were hurried annotations, written in a spidery hand. Even before she tried to puzzle them out, Mildred recognised the tiny marks and accents of Hungarian script, Anton's native tongue.

"Look at this," she murmured, drawing Bea's attention at once.

Bea peered over her shoulder. "Oh, it's sheet music. Is it from Anton's concerto?"

"It's possible," Mildred replied, holding the fragment up to the light. She could see that the margin had been savagely torn, as though ripped hastily from a larger document. But it was the notations that most drew her eye. Unlike typical rehearsal notes or tempo suggestions, these squiggles and words didn't fit any musical convention.

"Perhaps he was making a list of what to pack," Bea offered, undaunted by her lack of Hungarian. "Or… is that a recipe?"

Mildred allowed herself a soft chuckle. "Unlikely. Listen, this isn't musical instruction, and it's not performance marking either. The lines don't follow any bar structure, and see here? Where a rest should be, Anton's written the letter E three times, since, then followed it with a symbol…" She trailed off. "It's almost as if it's meant to confuse, or conceal something."

"A code!" Bea's eyes sparkled. "Like your crossword puzzles! Oh, Mildred, all is forgiven for dragging me out in the cold if I can play Watson to your Holmes."

"Perhaps." Mildred's brows drew together in concentration. The script was tiny, but the shapes and clusters seemed deliberate. Too neat for random jottings, yet too erratic for practical rehearsal notes. "See these clusters of letters, all separated by odd dots and lines? Hungarian, yes, but perhaps more than just language. A cipher of some kind."

She tucked the scrap discreetly into her notebook, flattening it between pages much as she had secret letters during the Armistice years. Her mind ticked through the possibilities—diaries encoded against prying eyes, secret correspondence, and the darker rumours of refugees smuggling their fortunes out of hostile lands concealed in the shape of music itself.

"We mustn't let Kent see this yet," she murmured, fierce with sudden certainty. "He won't see the significance, not until he's found his motive and his suspect in some tedious, linear fashion."

"Do you intend to solve this without him?" Bea asked, excitement warring with anxiety in her smile.

"Not entirely without him," Mildred allowed, voice low, "but I'll not let his procedures divert me from what I know to be a real clue. This is something Anton meant to hide, not only from his colleagues but from anyone who might discover the truth about that violin case."

The two women slipped out of the hall just as the first group of orchestra members returned for a debriefing with the concert committee. Outside, the day remained chilly, yet Mildred's thoughts raced with new warmth. She was reminded acutely of the cryptic will at Highfield and the sabotage at Brooklands. Patterns, codes, hidden meanings—all of which Kent, for all his dry competence and sardonic wit, too often dismissed at first glance.

On the steps, Bea linked arms with her. "You're plotting, Millie. I can always tell. That little frown and the way you thumb your notebook."

"Guilty as charged," Mildred agreed. As they crossed the broad steps, her head was already awash with possibilities. She would visit the reference room at the British Library, seek out Hungarian dictionaries, and perhaps, if necessary, consult a cryptanalyst from her old wartime circle.

They paused for a moment at the entrance, the city's energy surging all around them, oblivious to the cracks that violence had left in its cultural veneer. Mildred turned the scrap over once more. On the reverse, in a hasty scrawl, was a sequence of what looked more like mathematical figures than tempo markings: 2/7, 4/5, 14/3. A key, perhaps or merely the mad scribblings of a genius under pressure?

She would not allow the question to go unanswered.

That evening, beneath the amber glow of her bedside lamp, Mildred set to work. The page fluttered between her fingertips, foreign and yet marvellously familiar. She translated what little Hungarian she recalled from her Red Cross hospital days, puzzling out half-whispered phrases—"window", "gold", "movement",—all hinting at something hidden, something portable.

She murmured a few Latin phrases beneath her breath, another habit from harder times, as if those old incantations might unlock Anton's final secret.

Tomorrow, she decided, she would begin in earnest: with the musicologist at the museum perhaps, with an émigré community in Camden, with anyone who might recognise the true meaning of the notations on that furtive scrap. It was clear the violinist had lived with more to hide than a simple secret compartment. And it was equally clear, Inspector Kent's orders notwithstanding, that she could no more ignore this puzzle than breathe underwater.

Mildred smiled to herself, warm with the sense of purpose and the promise of a new challenge. She would follow the code, wherever it might lead, until the vanished violinist's last, cryptic message led her to the truth.

And if someone else, lurking in the London shadows, understood its meaning before she did—well, let them beware. Mildred Ramsay had never failed to bring light where it was most desperately needed.

With the city settling into its midnight hush, she closed her notebook over the mysterious scrap, utterly determined to see this case through to the end.

7

The elegant townhouse in Belgravia glowed with morning light, its drawing room already bustling with the cream of London society. Lady Ivy Carrington's breakfast salons were legendary—ostensibly gatherings for cultural discussion, but in reality, hotbeds of delicious gossip served alongside delicate pastries and perfectly brewed Darjeeling.

Mildred smoothed her dove-grey skirt as she and Bea were announced. Lady Ivy, resplendent in jade silk despite the early hour, swept toward them with outstretched hands.

"My dears! How absolutely thrilling that you've come. Everyone is positively agog about your presence at that dreadful concert. You simply must tell us everything."

Mildred exchanged a knowing glance with Bea. This was precisely why they had accepted the invitation—not for the mediocre scones, but for the unfiltered gossip that flowed as freely as the tea.

"Lady Ivy," Mildred replied with measured warmth, "how kind of you to include us. Though I'm afraid there's little to tell beyond what the newspapers have already reported."

"Nonsense!" Lady Ivy guided them toward a cluster of ladies by the window. "The papers never print the most interesting parts. Mrs Harcourt has taken to her bed with nerves, you know. Completely undone by the whole affair."

"Poor Sylvia," murmured a woman in lavender, whom Mildred recognised as the Countess of Westmorland. "Though I can't say I'm surprised. She's been looking positively haunted these past months."

"Financial troubles, I hear," whispered another lady behind her fan. "My husband says her investments have gone terribly wrong. Something about South American rubber that never materialised."

Mildred accepted a cup of tea, observing the circle with careful nonchalance. "I noticed she seemed rather agitated even before the performance began," she remarked.

This innocent observation unleashed a torrent of speculation.

"Well, of course she was agitated! Anton was threatening to break their contract," declared the Countess with authority. "My nephew works at the solicitor's firm that handles her affairs. He couldn't reveal details, naturally, but he did mention heated exchanges."

"And then there was that business in Vienna," added Lady Ivy, lowering her voice conspiratorially. "Anton was supposedly entangled with a baroness there—a married baroness, mind you—while under Sylvia's patronage. The scandal nearly ruined her standing among the artistic set."

"My dear, that's nothing compared to his affair with that Russian prima donna in Paris," countered a third woman, whose elaborate hat threatened the integrity of a nearby flower arrangement. "My husband's cousin attended a dinner where Anton appeared with her, though he was officially escorting Sylvia. She smiled through the entire evening, poor thing, but everyone knew."

Bea, who had been uncharacteristically quiet, suddenly brightened. "Speaking of escorts, I heard the most curious thing about Maestro Moretti. Apparently, he and Anton nearly came to blows during rehearsals last month."

All heads turned toward her, hungry for fresh information. Mildred marvelled at Bea's ability to redirect conversation with such artful precision.

"Do tell, Lady Beatrice!" Lady Ivy leaned forward eagerly.

"Oh, it's just something a little bird told me," Bea replied with practised modesty. "Apparently, Moretti accused Anton of deliberately altering tempos to showcase his virtuosity at the expense of the orchestra's cohesion. Called him a 'glory-seeking charlatan,' I believe."

This revelation prompted a new cascade of whispers. Mildred sipped her tea, mentally cataloguing each snippet of information. Truth often lay buried within exaggeration, waiting for a discerning ear to excavate it.

"Well, Moretti would say that, wouldn't he?" sniffed the Countess. "He's been green with envy since Monte Carlo."

"Monte Carlo?" Mildred inquired, her interest genuinely piqued.

"Oh, my dear, you didn't know?" Lady Ivy seized the opportunity to display her insider knowledge. "Last season, Moretti lost a small fortune at the tables there. Nearly ruined himself! And who should witness his humiliation but Anton Lanyi, who was performing at the casino that very night. They say Moretti had to borrow money from one of his patrons just to settle his hotel bill."

"How mortifying," Bea murmured sympathetically. "No wonder he resented Anton."

"Resentment enough to poison a man?" The question hung in the air, unspoken but palpable.

"Speaking of artistic rivalries," remarked the Countess, "did anyone see Edwin Sykes's review of Anton's Vienna performance last month? Positively venomous. Anton apparently confronted him at the Athenaeum Club, said something about critics who couldn't tell Mozart from Mahler without a programme note."

A young maid entered with fresh pastries, momentarily diverting attention. Bea caught Mildred's eye and nodded almost imperceptibly toward the servants' entrance. With a slight tilt of her head, Mildred acknowledged the silent suggestion.

As the gathering settled into smaller conversational clusters, Bea excused herself, ostensibly to powder her nose. Mildred knew better. Bea's uncanny ability to charm information from household staff had proved invaluable in their previous investigations. While society ladies might trade in half-truths and embellishments, servants observed with unfiltered clarity.

Left alone to navigate the salon, Mildred drifted toward a new group discussing the shock of Anton's collapse. She caught fragments that interested her: "...never seen anyone die so dramatically..." and "...wondered if it was part of the performance at first..."

Lady Ivy materialised at her elbow. "You seem deep in thought, Lady Mildred. Has our little gathering provided any clues for your investigation?"

Mildred raised an eyebrow. "My investigation, Lady Ivy? I'm

merely a concerned citizen who happened to witness a tragedy."

"Come now," Lady Ivy's smile was knowing. "After that business at Brooklands, you've quite the reputation as an amateur sleuth. Several of my guests specifically requested your presence today, hoping you might shed light on poor Anton's demise."

"I'm afraid I have no special insights to offer," Mildred replied diplomatically. "Inspector Kent is handling the matter with his usual thoroughness."

"Ah yes, the handsome inspector." Lady Ivy's eyes twinkled mischievously. "I've heard you two make quite the formidable team, despite your occasional... differences of opinion."

Before Mildred could formulate a suitably neutral response, Bea returned, her cheeks flushed with excitement that she was attempting, rather unsuccessfully, to conceal.

"Mildred, darling, I've just remembered we promised to meet Henry for lunch. We really shouldn't keep him waiting—you know how he fusses about punctuality."

Recognising the thinly veiled signal, Mildred nodded. "You're absolutely right. Lady Ivy, thank you for a most illuminating morning. Your gatherings are always so... informative."

Lady Ivy preened at what she took as a compliment. "Do come again, my dears. And if you happen to solve this little mystery, I expect to be the first to know!"

Outside in the crisp autumn air, Bea could barely contain herself. "Oh, Mildred, you won't believe what I've discovered! Lady Ivy's scullery maid is walking out with a footman from the Royal Albert Hall. And that footman happened to be polishing silver in the green room when Moretti arrived for the concert."

"And?" Mildred prompted as they turned onto a quieter street.

"And he was in a frightful state! Arrived with a man the footman didn't recognise—a burly fellow, looked foreign. They were arguing in Italian, but the footman understood enough to gather it was about money. A substantial sum, apparently."

Mildred considered this information. "A debt collector, perhaps?"

"That's what the footman thought. And here's the interesting part—Moretti kept saying something about 'after the performance' and 'when it's done.' The man eventually left, but not before Moretti promised him he'd have what he wanted by midnight."

"Midnight," Mildred echoed. "Well after Anton collapsed."

"Precisely!" Bea looked pleased with herself. "And there's more. The upstairs maid at Lady Ivy's has a cousin who works as a laundress for Mrs Harcourt. According to her, Sylvia was in tears the morning of the concert, burning papers in her bedroom fireplace."

They paused at a corner, waiting for a motor car to pass. Mildred's mind was already connecting these new details with her existing observations.

"Burning papers could suggest many things," she mused. "Evidence of financial troubles, perhaps, or correspondence she didn't want discovered."

"Or love letters," Bea suggested with characteristic romanticism. "Though that seems less likely given what we heard about Anton's continental dalliances."

As they walked, Mildred reflected on the morning's harvest of gossip and rumour. Beneath the embellishments and second-hand accounts lay kernels of truth more valuable than any formal testimony. People were careful about what they said to police inspectors but careless with their words at breakfast salons and in servants' halls.

"Do you think any of it connects to the scrap of music you found?" Bea asked, lowering her voice despite the empty street.

"I'm not sure yet," Mildred admitted. "But Moretti's gambling debts are interesting, especially if he was desperate enough to promise payment by midnight. And Sylvia's financial troubles align with what we observed at the concert—her whispered conversation with the solicitor about contracts and investigations."

They turned onto Eaton Square, where Henry would indeed be waiting for them, though their luncheon engagement had been more improvisation than fact.

"The question remains," Mildred continued, "how do these personal troubles connect to Anton's hidden compartment and coded music? Are we looking at a simple case of jealousy or desperation, or something larger?"

Bea adjusted her hat against a sudden gust of wind. "What did your Inspector Kent say about Moretti's gambling debts?"

"He's not 'my' Inspector," Mildred corrected automatically. "And I haven't shared this information with him yet. I'd prefer to have more concrete evidence before approaching him again. He was rather dismissive of my smuggling theory."

"Men can be so tediously literal," Bea sighed. "Though I suppose that's why they need us to illuminate the shadows they miss."

Mildred smiled at her friend's characterisation. "In fairness to Kent, he's working methodically with the evidence at hand. And without proof, my theories about coded music and smuggled valuables do sound rather fanciful."

"Then we shall simply have to find that proof," Bea declared with cheerful determination. "Starting with translating those Hungarian annotations. Have you made any progress?"

"Some," Mildred replied, patting her handbag where her notebook resided. "I've identified several recurring symbols that appear to be more numerical than linguistic. And the pattern of the notes themselves seems deliberate—almost like a cipher key."

They had reached the restaurant where Henry would be waiting, no doubt impatiently checking his pocket watch. Before entering, Mildred paused, her expression thoughtful.

"What strikes me most about this morning's gossip is how many people had reasons to resent Anton, yet how few had the specific knowledge and opportunity to poison him in such a particular way. The tonic bottle, the precise timing... that requires intimate familiarity with his habits."

"And access," Bea added. "Don't forget access."

"Indeed." Mildred nodded. "Someone close enough to doctor his tonic, someone who understood his routines."

As they stepped inside the warm restaurant, Mildred's mind continued to weave together the threads of gossip, evidence, and intuition. Each new detail added texture to the emerging picture: a celebrated violinist with secrets hidden in his instrument case, a circle of colleagues and patrons bound by ambition, resentment, and perhaps complicity, and at the centre, a coded message waiting to be deciphered.

What truths lay beneath the veneer of London's cultured society? And how many more secrets would she need to unearth before Anton's killer was brought to justice?

The answers, Mildred suspected, were hidden not just in the evidence Kent was gathering, but in the whispers that floated through drawing rooms and servant's halls—if only one knew how to listen.

8

Inspector Kent's office was heavy with the familiar scents of fresh ink, paraffin, and the faint, comforting dust of papers piled a decade high. Mildred stood by the window, gazing at the drizzle patterning the grimy panes, her posture as composed as ever, though her heartbeat tapped a brisker rhythm with every step the inspector took.

They had been here dozens of times before, if not in this precise room, then certainly at this juncture in one investigation or another: Mildred's sharp curiosity, Kent's dogged logic, and a corpse that refused to lie quietly.

Kent leafed through a sheaf of reports, his mouth set in that dry, analytical line Mildred knew so well. "We're making progress, Lady Mildred, despite the cabal of society gossips obfuscating every detail." He tapped a finger on the latest page. "The bulk of evidence is, as always, quite clear—jealousy, ambition, and money. Those are your motives."

Mildred resisted the urge to sigh, instead folding her gloved hands serenely. "Obvious motives are rarely the whole story, Inspector. If one could tie up a murder with a neat little bow every time jealousy surfaced, you'd need twice as many gaols."

Kent flashed her a sideways look. "Try telling that to every scorned heir or embittered spouse in London. Sylvia Harcourt's debts, Moretti's financial ruin, Nora's thwarted ambition—they're not merely window dressing. Anton Lanyi made enemies, and now he's dead. Motives, means, opportunity. That's police work."

Mildred held his gaze, refusing to be cowed. "You're looking for a single cause. A broken heart, a ruined reputation, a pile of lost wagers. But have you truly considered the violin case itself—the hollow compartment, the coded scrap of music?" She let her voice carry just a hint of challenge, tempered by the familiar dance of their rivalry. "You found nothing in the hidden space, did you?"

Kent crossed to the fire and placed his hands behind his back. "Nothing but dust and velvet. There's no proof of anything grander than an instrument case modified for spare strings or love notes. You're reaching. You want conspiracy. But this is a murder born of resentment and desperation, not international intrigue."

Mildred moved to the desk, careful to set her reticule down with precision. "And yet Anton's history suggests otherwise. He travelled Europe with rare freedom after the war, moving between borders no one else could cross with ease. There are rumours—"

"Always rumours." Kent's tone was sharper now. "Always an exotic theory with you, Lady Mildred. I appreciate speculation as much as the next detective—so long as it's anchored to the facts."

Mildred took out her small notebook, flicking to a page marked with annotations and sketches of Anton's violin case.

She tapped a line with her pencil. "A violin case lined and partitioned especially. Not a family heirloom, not a standard commission. And the music scrap—Hungarian annotations, numbers, and clusters that make no musical sense."

Kent cut in, perhaps a shade too swiftly. "We've been over this. Volkov admits to making the compartment. It was Anton's paranoia; he thought his scores might be stolen. Nothing in it now."

"Or someone emptied it in haste during the confusion," Mildred pressed. She leaned forward, her eyes bright. "You're missing the web, Inspector. The way Anton grew nervous these past weeks, the whispered quarrels, the abrupt desire to break his patron-contract with Sylvia Harcourt. All of it—"

He lifted a hand to halt her. "You see patterns everywhere. It's starting to look rather desperate, I must say. Moretti is broke, unable to pay his Monte Carlo losses. Otto was pressed for loans by Anton. Nora was promised the solo and then denied it. Sylvia's reputation would collapse if word spread about her finances. Each of them stood to gain by getting Anton out of their way. That's not a web. That's a circle."

"Circles can be webs, Inspector, if you pick at the threads."

The silence crackled. Mildred recognised the set of his jaw—a signal that he was circling the wagons, closing ranks around established procedure. She cast her mind back to the previous morning's society gossip: the burning of papers, the missing hour between Anton's pre-concert routine and his arrival onstage, Bea's report from the servants' hall about Moretti's foreign visitor. None of it neat, none of it tidily explained by plain old jealousy or bills of exchange.

She fixed Kent with a direct stare. "Are you so certain, Charles, that you're not missing something vital because its shape is inconvenient?"

There it was—the smallest flicker in his eyes, as frustration simmered beneath his reserve. "I am certain of this: you're not part of the official enquiry. You cannot go nosing about evidence, nor may you conduct interviews under the guise of society chit-chat. You've helped, yes—more than once now. But there are boundaries, Lady Mildred, and you're on the edge."

Something in his warning struck a nerve. Her voice dropped, steady and fierce. "You think I care for boundaries, when the innocent are suspected and the guilty slip away? You called me for my observations. Are you now dismissing them because they're not on the proper forms?"

Kent raked a hand through his hair, a gesture rare enough to betray the depth of his exasperation. He stepped closer, lowering his voice conspiratorially. "What if you're wrong? What if you cause greater harm with a wild goose chase? I have men to command, a career to salvage, laws to uphold—"

"And what if you're wrong, Inspector? What if Anton's death is more than a temper or an unpaid debt? What if secrets cross the Channel in a violin case, and what if someone paid dearly to keep those secrets hidden?" Her voice glowed with quiet anger. "I have as much cause as you to see justice done."

They stared at one another, two persistent minds under the shifting light of suspicion and obligation.

"Stay away from this one, Mildred." Kent's words were soft but iron-bound, his meaning unmistakable. "I'm serious. The higher-ups are watching, and I cannot protect you if you stray again."

That, at last, put her on her mettle. She straightened, chin lifted, the old stubborn glint in her eye. "Thank you for the warning, Inspector. I promise to give it every consideration."

He looked like he wanted to say more—perhaps something gentler, more personal—but professionalism clamped his lips shut. She snatched her reticule, calm and poised as ever.

At the door, Mildred paused, her gloved fingertips barely grazing the wood. "I appreciate your dedication, Charles. But I can't put aside what I've seen and I don't intend to."

With that, she slipped from the room, heart pounding not with fear but with determination. Outside, the bustle of Scotland Yard seemed to part for her. The coded scrap of music inside her notebook was warm from her touch—a small, stubborn seed of mystery.

Let Kent chase after debts and betrayals if he must. Mildred Ramsay would follow the notes, even to the shadows the inspector refused to enter.

Unbeknownst to both, a shadow peeled itself from the alcove beneath the stairs, someone else had overheard the exchange, and their interest in secrets and hidden compartments might prove even more dangerous than either Kent or Mildred supposed.

The web of intrigue was growing. And Mildred, shut out by authority, was about to venture further in.

9

Morning fog hung like a theatre curtain over the narrow streets of Camden, transforming ordinary houses into ghostly silhouettes. Mildred and Beatrice walked arm in arm, their breath forming small clouds as they navigated the winding lanes. The address they sought was tucked away on a side street, far from the elegant neighbourhoods they typically frequented.

"Are you quite certain this is wise?" Bea asked, stepping delicately around a puddle. "Inspector Kent was rather emphatic about us staying out of his investigation."

Mildred's expression remained serene, though her eyes held a glint of determination. "We're merely paying a social call on a celebrated craftsman, Bea. There's no law against admiring fine violins."

"No, but there might be something against nosing about a murder investigation after being expressly warned off," Bea replied with a wry smile. "Though I must admit, I do adore a bit of intrigue before luncheon."

They turned a final corner and found themselves before a modest shopfront. A weathered wooden sign hung above the door, bearing the simple words *'Volkov – Luthier'* in faded gold lettering. Through the grimy window, they could glimpse the shadowy outlines of violins and cellos, suspended like elegant phantoms.

"Remember," Mildred murmured as she raised her gloved hand to the door, "we're here out of appreciation for the craft. Nothing more."

Bea nodded, arranging her features into an expression of innocent enthusiasm. "I shall be the very picture of wide-eyed admiration."

A small bell tinkled as they entered, announcing their presence to the empty shop. The air inside was heavy with the scents of varnish, wood shavings, and beeswax. Instruments in various stages of completion hung from hooks or rested on workbenches. In the corner, a small samovar sat cold atop a cabinet.

"Hello?" Mildred called softly. "Mr Volkov?"

A rustling sound came from behind a curtained doorway, followed by the scrape of a chair. A moment later, a man emerged, wiping his hands on a cloth. Sergei Volkov was tall and lean, with silver-streaked dark hair and the deep-set eyes of someone who spent hours focusing on minute details. He regarded the two women with visible surprise.

"Ladies," he said, his accent thick but his English precise. "This is unexpected. How may I help you?"

Mildred stepped forward with a warm smile. "Mr Volkov, I'm Lady Mildred Ramsay, and this is my friend, Lady Beatrice Mortimer. We hope you don't mind our intrusion, but we've heard such wonderful things about your craftsmanship."

Volkov's expression remained guarded, his dark eyes assessing them. "It is unusual for ladies of your standing to visit a workshop such as mine. Most prefer to admire instruments in concert halls, not surrounded by sawdust and glue pots."

"Oh, but that's precisely what makes it so fascinating!" Bea exclaimed, moving toward a half-finished violin with genuine curiosity. "To see how these marvellous instruments come to life. It's like magic, isn't it, Mildred?"

"Indeed," Mildred agreed, watching Volkov carefully. "We were at the Royal Albert Hall on the night of Anton Lanyi's performance. His playing was extraordinary, as was his instrument. We later learned you were the craftsman responsible for its care."

At the mention of Anton's name, something flickered across Volkov's face—a tightening around the eyes, perhaps, or a momentary tension in his shoulders. "Anton's Guarneri del Gesù was a magnificent violin. One of the finest I've handled in thirty years of work."

"You must have known him well," Mildred ventured, moving deeper into the shop to examine a row of violin cases. "To care for such a valuable instrument requires great trust."

Volkov's lips pressed into a thin line. "We were countrymen of a sort. Both displaced by war and politics. He trusted my hands with his livelihood."

"And how tragic that his final performance was cut short so dramatically," Bea added, her voice dropping to a suitably hushed tone. "Were you in attendance that night, Mr Volkov?"

"No," he replied shortly. "I had work. Many instruments need attention."

As Volkov moved to retrieve a violin from Bea's eager hands, Mildred noticed a curious detail. Around his right wrist, partially concealed by his shirt cuff, was a ring of bruising, the colour suggesting it was several days old. When he reached up to adjust a hanging cello, his sleeve rode higher, revealing more marks.

"This cello is particularly beautiful," Mildred commented, deliberately drawing his attention away from Bea, who had begun to wander toward the curtained doorway. "Is it a commission?"

"Yes. For a gentleman in Vienna." Volkov carefully repositioned the instrument. "A belated birthday gift for his daughter."

While Volkov described the cello's unique features, Mildred kept one eye on Bea, who had casually pushed the curtain aside just enough to peer into the back room. After a moment, Bea turned and caught Mildred's eye, giving an almost imperceptible nod.

"Mr Volkov," Mildred said suddenly, "I couldn't help but notice Anton's violin case had some unusual features. Was that also your handiwork?"

The change was immediate. Volkov's shoulders stiffened, and his expression closed like a door slammed shut. "I repair instruments, Lady Mildred. Cases are merely containers."

"Yet Anton's case was rather special, wasn't it?" Mildred pressed gently. "With its hidden compartment and unique mechanism?"

Volkov set down his polishing cloth with deliberate care. "Why have you really come here? You are not interested in violins."

Bea rejoined them, her usual cheer slightly forced. "Oh, but we are! Though I must confess, I'm absolutely hopeless at any instrument. I once tried learning the piano, but my teacher gave up after three lessons. Said I sounded like a cat walking across the keyboard!"

Her cheerful prattle drew a reluctant smile from Volkov, though his eyes remained wary.

"Mr Volkov," Mildred continued, her tone softening, "we admired Anton's artistry. His death was shocking, and we simply wish to understand what happened. The case seemed... significant."

Volkov hesitated, then gestured toward two simple wooden chairs. "Please. Sit. I will make tea."

While he disappeared behind the curtain, Bea leaned close to Mildred. "There's a room back there with a small bed. On the table, I saw several very expensive bottles of wine. French, I believe, and what looked like a train timetable for the Continent."

Mildred nodded, filing away this information. When Volkov returned with a tray bearing three glasses in silver holders, she accepted hers with a gracious smile.

"This is very kind, Mr Volkov. Russian tea, I presume?"

He inclined his head. "My one luxury from home."

They sipped in silence for a moment, the fragrant tea warming them against the chill of the shop. Finally, Volkov spoke, his voice low and measured.

"What you ask about, the case, it was a commission. Anton was... particular about his things."

"Particular enough to require a secret compartment?" Mildred inquired.

Volkov sighed heavily. "Musicians are superstitious people, Lady Mildred. Some carry lucky charms, others specific rosin, or a favourite baton. Anton carried letters. Private correspondence he did not wish to lose in hotel rooms or backstage areas. He asked for a secure place within his case."

"Letters?" Bea echoed, her eyebrows rising. "How romantic! From a sweetheart, perhaps?"

Volkov shrugged. "He did not share their contents with me. I merely built what he requested."

Mildred studied the luthier's face, searching for signs of deception. "And the mechanism to open it... that was quite elaborate for storing simple letters."

"It was what he wanted. He paid well for the work." Volkov's hands cradled his tea glass, the bruises on his wrist now clearly visible. Noticing Mildred's gaze, he tugged his sleeve down self-consciously.

"Those look painful," she observed quietly. "A workshop accident?"

Something darkened in Volkov's eyes. "Yes. A clamp slipped," he said too quickly. The imprint on his wrist looked more like fingers than iron.

It was a lie, and they both knew it. The pattern of bruising suggested fingers, not the clean line of a woodworking tool.

Bea, meandering around the shop again, paused before a display of violin bows. "These are exquisite! Do you make them as well?"

Grateful for the distraction, Volkov rose to join her. "No, those come from a specialist in Paris. The balance must be perfect—too heavy at the frog, and the sound is dull; too light, and control is lost."

While Bea kept Volkov engaged with questions about different types of wood and horsehair, Mildred examined the workshop more carefully. Near the samovar, a small stack of papers caught her eye—invoices, mostly in Russian, but with figures clearly visible. The amounts were substantial, far exceeding what one might expect for routine repairs or even custom work.

Glancing back to ensure Volkov was still occupied with Bea's enthusiastic inquiries, Mildred silently moved closer to the papers. Among them was a torn envelope addressed to Volkov, with the return address in Budapest. The postmark was dated just three days before Anton's death.

"Mr Volkov," she called, drawing his attention back. "Were you working on any special projects for Anton before his death? Beyond the case, I mean."

The luthier's face remained impassive, but his fingers curled slightly against his palm. "Anton was always seeking perfection. Small adjustments to his instrument, a different bridge, experiments with strings. Nothing unusual."

"And when did you last see him?"

Volkov hesitated, just a fraction too long. "A week before the concert. He brought his violin for final adjustments before the performance."

"How conscientious," Bea remarked. "I imagine such a valuable instrument requires constant attention."

"Like a temperamental child," Volkov agreed with a thin smile. "Always demanding, never satisfied."

Mildred set down her empty glass. "We've taken enough of your time, Mr Volkov. Thank you for the tea and conversation. Your workshop is fascinating."

Relief washed over his features, though he maintained his composure. "You are welcome. Though I'm afraid I have told you nothing that would help understand Anton's tragedy."

As they prepared to leave, Mildred paused by a violin case similar to Anton's. "You mentioned letters in the hidden compartment. Nothing else? No valuables or documents?"

Volkov's expression hardened. "I told you what I know, Lady Mildred. Anton wanted a compartment; I built it. What he kept there was his business."

"Of course," Mildred replied smoothly. "Forgive my curiosity. It just seemed an elaborate precaution for ordinary correspondence."

"These are not ordinary times, Lady Mildred," Volkov said quietly. "For those of us who fled our homes with nothing, even letters become precious beyond measure."

There was truth in his words, but Mildred sensed layers beneath—complications and evasions that spoke of deeper involvements. As they bid the luthier goodbye and stepped back into the misty street, Bea linked her arm through Mildred's again.

"Well?" she prompted once they were safely out of earshot. "What do you make of our Russian friend?"

"He's hiding something," Mildred replied thoughtfully. "Those bruises weren't from any workshop accident. Someone has been rough with him, and recently. And did you notice how he tensed when I mentioned the compartment?"

"Indeed! And those wine bottles in the back room were quite expensive for a humble craftsman. Château something-or-other—I couldn't quite see the label."

They walked in silence for a moment, each processing what they had learned.

"He admitted to building the secret compartment," Mildred finally said. "That confirms my suspicion that it was deliberate, not a quirk of construction as Kent suggested. But letters? I'm not convinced."

"Nor I," Bea agreed. "Why would Anton need such an elaborate hiding place for ordinary correspondence? And why would Mr Volkov have marks on his wrists that look suspiciously like someone grabbed him rather forcefully?"

As they reached the main road and hailed a cab, Mildred's thoughts returned to the scrap of music hidden in her notebook, with its curious Hungarian annotations and mathematical figures. Somehow, it all connected. Anton's hidden compartment, Volkov's bruises, the expensive wine, and the coded sheet music.

"I think," she said carefully as they settled into the cab, "that our luthier knows far more about Anton's activities than he's willing to admit. And whatever was hidden in that violin case was valuable enough for someone to kill for."

"And the same someone may have visited Mr Volkov to ensure his silence," Bea added, her usual light-heartedness momentarily subdued.

The cab rattled through the clearing fog, taking them back toward Mayfair and the comfortable world they knew. But Mildred's mind remained in that dusty workshop, puzzling over what Volkov had revealed and what he had so carefully concealed.

What exactly had Anton been hiding in that compartment? And how many others might be implicated in whatever scheme had ultimately cost him his life? The questions multiplied, each one leading deeper into a mystery that seemed to grow more complex with every new discovery.

One thing was certain: Inspector Kent would not approve of today's excursion. But as the cab turned onto Piccadilly, Mildred found herself more determined than ever to uncover the truth, with or without the inspector's blessing.

10

A chill autumn fog settled over London as Mildred made her way towards the Royal College of Music. The imposing stone building loomed through the mist like a watchful sentinel, its windows reflecting the weak morning light. Inside, Mildred knew, she would find Nora Bellamy—the young violinist whose ambition and proximity to Anton Lanyi had already made her an object of whispers and sidelong glances.

The corridors echoed with muffled scales and arpeggios; the sounds bleeding together into an oddly discordant symphony. Mildred followed the building's winding passages, guided by the desk porter's vague directions. She found Nora in a small practice room, alone save for her violin and the ghost of unrealised ambitions.

Mildred paused at the threshold. The young woman sat hunched on a worn bench, her instrument beside her, tears tracking silently down her pale cheeks. Her posture spoke of defeat, her shoulders curved inward as if to protect herself from the world's judgement.

"Miss Bellamy?" Mildred said softly, knocking lightly on the half-open door.

Nora started hastily wiping her face with her handkerchief. "Lady Mildred! I—I didn't expect visitors." She attempted to compose herself, smoothing her skirt with unsteady fingers.

"Forgive the intrusion," Mildred replied, stepping into the room. "I thought we might speak privately, away from the speculation and gossip that seems to have consumed London this week."

Nora's gaze darted nervously to the doorway, as if expecting accusers to materialise. "Everyone is talking about me, aren't they? About how I... how I might have..."

"People always talk," Mildred said calmly, settling onto the bench beside Nora. "But I prefer to listen directly to those involved."

Nora stared at her hands, which twisted her handkerchief into a crumpled knot. "What can I tell you that would make any difference? The papers have already decided I'm either a scorned lover or a ruthless opportunist."

"The papers rarely capture the truth of anything, in my experience," Mildred observed. "I'd rather hear about your relationship with Anton from you."

For a moment, Nora remained silent, the only sound the distant echo of a cello's melancholy voice. Then, haltingly, she began to speak.

"He promised me a solo," she whispered, her voice catching. "In the charity concert. He said I was ready, that my interpretation of the Mendelssohn adagio had 'soul beyond technique.' He announced it at rehearsal. Everyone heard him." Her fingers worried her handkerchief to creases. "I practised for weeks. Sixteen hours a day, until my fingers bled and Moretti complained about my 'obsessive monopoly' of the rehearsal spaces."

"And then?" Mildred prompted gently.

"Three days before the concert, he changed his mind." Nora's voice hardened with remembered hurt. "No explanation, no apology. Just 'Plans have changed, my dear. Perhaps next season.' As if my career, my moment, was nothing but an afterthought."

The raw pain in her voice was unmistakable. Mildred watched her carefully, noting the genuine emotion but also the flash of anger that accompanied it. Ambition thwarted could fester into resentment. Even the most gentle soul might harbour darker impulses when humiliated.

"Did you confront him about it?" Mildred asked.

"Confront Anton Lanyi?" Nora gave a brittle laugh. "One doesn't 'confront' the maestro. But I did ask him why. Just once, very quietly, after rehearsal." She closed her eyes briefly. "He seemed distracted, almost afraid. Said something vague about 'complications' and 'when things settle.' Then Otto called him away for a private word, and that was the last conversation we ever had."

"How did the others react to your demotion?" Mildred inquired, keeping her tone conversational.

"Moretti seemed pleased; he never thought I was ready. Sylvia Harcourt barely acknowledged it; she was too busy whispering with her solicitor. Otto just watched, as he watches everything, saying nothing." Nora shrugged wearily. "The rest of the orchestra were kind enough not to mention it to my face."

Mildred nodded thoughtfully. Each reaction revealed its own complexities: Moretti's professional jealousy, Sylvia's distraction, Otto's inscrutable vigilance. Any of them might hide darker motives beneath their apparent indifference.

"Inspector Kent has been asking about your tonic, I understand," Mildred said, changing direction.

Nora's face paled. With shaking hands, she reached into her satchel and withdrew a small dark-glass apothecary bottle. "This. It's nothing but herbal drops for nerves. Every musician has something—some drink, some smoke, some pray. I take three drops before performances." Her voice grew desperate. "He keeps asking if I gave any to Anton, if I had access to his dressing room. I didn't! I would never—"

"May I?" Mildred held out her hand. Nora hesitated, then passed over the bottle.

It was unremarkable: dark glass with a faded label reading *'Tonikum'* in Gothic script. A paper insert, yellowed with age, bore dosage instructions in Hungarian. The seal was unbroken, the liquid within was a pale amber when held to the light.

"My aunt sends it from Budapest," Nora explained. "It's just valerian and lime flower, perhaps a touch of camphor. Nothing sinister."

Mildred turned the bottle carefully, studying it from every angle. "And yet in the current climate, even the most innocent item becomes suspect."

"Exactly!" Nora's relief at being understood was palpable. "The inspector looked at me as if I'd been caught red-handed, merely for having nerve tonic. As though half the orchestra doesn't carry similar remedies!"

A thought occurred to Mildred. "Did Anton use a tonic before performances?"

Nora nodded. "Always. A Hungarian preparation, darker than mine. He was quite superstitious about it. Three drops, precisely five minutes before going on stage. Otto would prepare it for him sometimes."

"Otto?" Mildred kept her voice carefully neutral.

"Yes, they had a routine. Otto would pass Anton the bottle while he adjusted his cuffs. Anton always uncorked it himself, took the drops, and Otto would return the bottle to its velvet pouch. Like a ritual for luck."

Mildred made a mental note of this detail. The tonic bottle she had seen near Anton's body matched this description. If the poison had been administered through the tonic, Otto's regular access presented an opportunity—though, of course, so did Nora's familiarity with such preparations.

"And Maestro Moretti? Was he nearby during these pre-performance rituals?" Mildred asked.

"Usually pacing and muttering about tempos," Nora replied with the ghost of a smile. "He and Anton argued constantly about interpretation. Anton preferred to take more liberties with the score than Moretti thought proper."

"And Mrs Harcourt?"

"Sometimes she would visit backstage with well-wishers or potential donors. She liked to show off her 'discovery,' as she called Anton." A trace of bitterness crept into Nora's voice. "Though recently, she seemed more anxious than proud when she brought visitors around."

Each new detail added layers to Mildred's understanding—not only of Anton's final moments but of the complex web of relationships surrounding him. Moretti's artistic frustration, Sylvia's financial concerns, Otto's intimate access, and Nora's crushed aspirations—all potential motives, all impossible to dismiss.

Nora seemed to read something in Mildred's expression. "You think I did it, don't you? That's why you're here."

"I'm here because I believe in understanding before judging," Mildred replied evenly. "And because I've seen how easily suspicion can attach itself to the most vulnerable person in a room."

Nora's eyes filled with fresh tears. "I admired him, Lady Mildred. Even when he took away my chance, I admired his genius. I would never have harmed him."

The sincerity in her voice was compelling, yet Mildred had learned from experience that the most genuine emotions could coexist with desperate actions. Nora's hurt was real but so was her ambition. So was the bottle of tonic that could, with minimal effort, be twisted into damning evidence.

"May I keep this for safekeeping?" Mildred asked, indicating the bottle. "I fear it might be misinterpreted if it remains in your possession."

Relief washed over Nora's face. "Please. Take it. I can't bear the way Inspector Kent looks at it, at me, as though he's already decided my guilt."

As Mildred carefully tucked the bottle into her handbag, she noted how Nora's grip had eased at last. Was it simply relief at having someone listen, or the subtler calm of having successfully shifted suspicion elsewhere?

"If you recall anything else about that evening—anything unusual in Anton's behaviour, or in those around him—please let me know," Mildred said, rising to leave.

"I will." Nora hesitated, then added, "Lady Mildred? Do you think they'll ever let me play again? After all this?"

The vulnerability in the question touched Mildred's heart. "Talent finds its audience eventually, Miss Bellamy. And scandals fade more quickly than true ability."

Outside in the corridor, Mildred found Bea waiting, her curiosity barely contained. "Well? Is she our poisoner, or merely a convenient scapegoat?"

Mildred considered her words carefully. "She's a young woman with crushed dreams and a bottle of tonic that looks remarkably similar to Anton's. Whether that makes her a murderer or simply unfortunate remains to be seen."

"You don't sound convinced either way," Bea observed shrewdly.

"Because I'm not," Mildred admitted. "Nora had motive, certainly. But so did Moretti with his artistic frustration, Sylvia with her financial troubles, and Otto with his mysterious access to Anton's preparations."

They descended the broad staircase, their footsteps echoing on marble. Bea lowered her voice despite the empty corridor. "Which of them do you favour, then? For the crime?"

Mildred shook her head slightly. "It's too early to eliminate anyone. Each has shadows in their story, and each had opportunity in different ways. What concerns me most is that the simplest explanation, a jealous understudy with a convenient bottle of tonic, may be precisely what someone is counting on."

As they stepped out into the foggy London morning, Mildred couldn't shake the feeling that they were being observed. A tall figure in a dark coat stood beneath a distant lamppost, collar turned up against the chill. For a moment, their gazes met across the square, then the fog swirled, and the watcher melted away into the grey veil of the city.

Who among Anton's circle was desperate enough to silence him forever? And who among them might now be watching Mildred's own investigation with growing concern? The answer lay buried somewhere in the tangle of ambition, secrets, and music—a deadly composition still building toward its final, revealing chord.

11

The rehearsal hall of the Royal Philharmonic Society rang with Mozart's music, as strings and woodwinds played together under Maestro Giulio Moretti's strict baton. Mildred and Bea had secured seats in the otherwise empty audience, their presence tolerated only because Lady Ivy Carrington, a society patron whose financial contributions bought latitude even in the most exclusive artistic circles, had arranged it.

"I still don't see why we're watching a rehearsal when there's a perfectly good tea shop around the corner," Bea whispered, suppressing a yawn. "Musicians practising is like watching paint dry, only with more dramatic grimacing."

Mildred smiled faintly but kept her attention fixed on Moretti. The Italian conductor stood rigid on his podium, his thin frame vibrating with barely contained energy as he guided the orchestra through a passage. Something in his demeanour suggested a storm brewing beneath the surface—shoulders tense, mouth set in a grim line, eyes flashing whenever a musician missed a cue.

"Watch him," Mildred murmured. "He's wound tighter than Henry's pocket watch."

Indeed, even as she spoke, Moretti's composure began to crack. He rapped his baton sharply against the music stand, silencing the orchestra mid-phrase.

"No, no, NO!" His voice sliced through the stillness, accent thickening with emotion. "The phrasing is all wrong. This passage requires subtlety! It is not some hackneyed carnival tune!"

The first violinist, a grey-haired man who had taken Nora's place as leader since Anton's death, attempted to interject. "Maestro, perhaps if we—"

"Perhaps if you played as written!" Moretti cut him off, brandishing his baton like a sword. "Anton would never have tolerated such mediocrity. He understood nuance, at least when he chose to!"

A ripple of discomfort passed through the musicians. Anton's name had become a spectre in their midst, invoked rarely and with caution.

"Of course," Moretti continued, his voice dripping with bitterness, "when it suited him, he would discard the composer's intentions entirely. Do you know what he did in Vienna last month? He replaced Mozart's original cadenza with his own composition! His own! As if Mozart required improvement!"

Moretti's face had flushed a dangerous scarlet. He slammed his score shut with such force that several musicians flinched.

"He stole my cadenzas too," he seethed, seemingly oblivious to his increasingly uncomfortable audience. "Three years of work. My interpretations, my artistry—all appropriated without acknowledgment! And for what? So the great Anton

Lanyi could bask in yet more adulation while the rest of us languished in his shadow!"

From the back of the hall came a soft cough. Inspector Kent stood in the doorway, notebook in hand, his keen gaze fixed on the conductor's outburst. Beside him, a uniformed constable shifted uncomfortably.

Moretti froze, suddenly aware of his public display. He straightened, adjusting his cuffs with affected nonchalance. "We shall take a fifteen-minute recess," he announced coldly. "When we return, I expect precision."

As the musicians gratefully dispersed, Kent made his way down the aisle toward Moretti, nodding briefly to Mildred and Bea as he passed. The inspector's interest in Moretti's tirade was palpable. A new thread to pull in his methodical investigation.

"Maestro Moretti," Kent began, his tone deceptively casual, "I couldn't help overhearing your remarks about Mr Lanyi. It seems there was considerable tension between you."

Moretti's chin lifted defensively. "Professional disagreements only, Inspector. Common in artistic circles."

"Professional disagreements that caused you to describe him as a thief of your work?" Kent pressed. "That sounds rather personal."

Mildred watched the exchange with interest. Kent was circling Moretti like a chess player identifying a weakness, his questions seemingly innocuous yet deliberately aimed to provoke.

"Anton Lanyi was a brilliant violinist," Moretti conceded stiffly, "but he had an unfortunate tendency to... borrow liberally from colleagues. It was professionally frustrating, nothing more."

"Frustrating enough to confront him about it?" Kent inquired.

"Of course I confronted him! What self-respecting artist wouldn't? But that hardly makes me a murderer, Inspector."

Kent smiled thinly. "I don't recall suggesting it did, Maestro."

The trap had been neatly sprung. Moretti's face darkened as he realised he had overplayed his hand. "If you'll excuse me, I must prepare for the second half of rehearsal."

As the conductor stalked away, Kent turned to Mildred and Bea. "Lady Mildred, Lady Beatrice. I should have known you'd be here."

Bea beamed at him. "We're becoming quite musical lately, Inspector. Practically virtuosos of eavesdropping."

Kent's lips twitched, but he maintained his professional demeanour. "And what brings you to this particular rehearsal? More innocent curiosity?"

"We're here at Lady Ivy's invitation," Mildred replied smoothly. "She's considering increasing her patronage and wanted opinions on the orchestra's quality post-Anton."

"How convenient," Kent observed dryly. "And did you find Maestro Moretti's outburst illuminating?"

Mildred considered her words carefully. "It was certainly passionate. Whether it illuminates your case depends on how you interpret such passion."

"Indeed? And how would you interpret it, Lady Mildred? Since you're developing such expertise in criminal psychology."

The subtle challenge in his voice was familiar territory in their ongoing intellectual sparring. Mildred accepted it with a small smile.

"I'd say his anger is genuine, certainly. The question is whether it represents the slow boil of premeditated hatred or merely the flash fire of artistic temperament."

"An interesting distinction," Kent mused. "And your conclusion?"

Mildred glanced toward where Moretti stood, gesticulating forcefully to a violinist. "His rage is noisy, Inspector. Calculated hatred tends to whisper, not shout."

Kent's eyebrow rose. "Poetic, but hardly conclusive. Moretti had motive—professional jealousy, artistic theft—and opportunity. He was backstage throughout the evening."

"As were a dozen others," Mildred pointed out. "Including those whose motives might be less obvious but far more compelling."

Before Kent could respond, the musicians began returning to their seats. The inspector tucked his notebook away with a nod of acknowledgement.

"We'll continue this discussion another time, Lady Mildred. For now, enjoy the music. What remains of it after Maestro Moretti's passionate interpretations."

As Kent departed, Bea leaned closer to Mildred. "Well? Do you think our temperamental Italian did it? He certainly has the dramatic flair for a good poisoning."

Mildred watched Moretti ascend his podium once more, his movements precise and controlled now that he knew official eyes were upon him.

"I'm not certain," she admitted quietly. "His outburst seemed genuine. The festering resentment of a proud man who felt diminished by Anton's success. But there's something performative about it too. Almost as if he wants us to see his anger."

"A decoy," Bea suggested, eyes widening. "How deliciously cunning! Make himself the obvious suspect so we overlook someone else."

"Or," Mildred countered, "evidence of genuine wrongdoing. Sometimes the most obvious answer is correct."

They fell silent as Moretti raised his baton, and the orchestra launched into Mozart's delicate phrases once more. Mildred studied the conductor's every gesture, searching for clues in the fluid movement of his hands, the intensity of his gaze, the set of his shoulders.

What struck her most was the subtle transformation. Where moments before he had been a volcano of rage, now he was precision and control incarnate—passion channelled into perfect musical discipline. It was an impressive display of self-mastery, and oddly disquieting.

Could a man capable of such swift emotional regulation also be capable of meticulous murder? Could the same hands that coaxed such beauty from an orchestra have delivered poison with calculating precision? Or was his very visibility, his noisy, public antagonism, proof of his innocence?

As the music swelled around them, Mildred found herself caught between competing theories. Moretti certainly had motive; professional jealousy intensified by Anton's alleged theft of his work. According to Lady Ivy's gossip, he also had financial pressures from his gambling losses in Monte Carlo, which Anton had witnessed. His position as conductor gave him access to the backstage area and potentially to Anton's tonic.

Yet something still felt wrong. Mildred had encountered enough murderers—at Highfield Manor and Brooklands—to recognise that the most dangerous ones rarely advertised their grievances. They cultivated quiet smiles while nursing silent rage. Moretti's anger was explosive, theatrical, almost cathartic, the opposite of the cold calculation required to poison a man in the midst of a crowded concert hall.

Unless that was precisely the point.

The thought struck her with sudden clarity. What better way to deflect suspicion than to present oneself as too obvious a suspect? Too passionate to be capable of the patient plotting that poisoning required? Perhaps Moretti's outburst was not evidence of innocence but a carefully calibrated performance designed to make investigators discount him.

She recalled something Henry had said during the Brooklands investigation: "The best place to hide is often in plain sight."

The music reached its crescendo, Moretti's body arching with the final triumphant chord. As the last note faded, Mildred made a mental note to examine the conductor's movements more carefully. Where had he been in the crucial minutes before Anton took the stage? Who had seen him, and where? Had he ever handled Anton's tonic bottle?

These questions would need answers before she could dismiss Moretti from her list of suspects or elevate him to its top position. For now, she would watch and listen, gathering threads that might eventually weave together into the pattern of truth.

As the musicians began to pack away their instruments, Bea nudged Mildred gently. "Penny for your thoughts? You've gone all mysterious and pensive again."

Mildred smiled. "I was just considering the nature of performance, Bea. Musicians spend their lives practising deception of a sort. Making difficult passages seem effortless, concealing their true emotions behind the mask of the music."

"Rather like murderers," Bea observed with unexpected astuteness. "Though I suppose murderers rarely get standing ovations."

"No," Mildred agreed softly, watching as Moretti descended from his podium with the graceful precision of a man accustomed to commanding attention. "But the best of them believe they deserve one."

As they gathered their things to leave, Mildred noticed a small, crumpled piece of paper that had fallen from Moretti's score during his earlier outburst. It lay forgotten near the conductor's stand, a discarded fragment of what appeared to be a letter.

With casual deliberation, she steered Bea toward it, then knelt to adjust her shoe, palming the paper in one swift movement. Only when they were safely outside did she examine her find, a torn corner of notepaper bearing a single line in what appeared to be Anton's flowing script:

"If you speak of our arrangement to anyone, remember that you have far more to lose than I."

The cryptic warning sent a chill through Mildred. What arrangement had existed between Anton and Moretti? And who indeed had more to lose—the now-dead virtuoso, or the maestro who had so publicly proclaimed his grievances?

As they left the rehearsal hall, Mildred noticed Edwin Sykes lurking near the stage door, notebook in hand. The critic's thin face brightened with malicious interest at Moretti's tirade. "Trouble in the artistic paradise?" he inquired, his pen poised. "I always said Lanyi was more showman than musician. My readers appreciate honesty, you know."

"Your readers appreciate cruelty packaged as insight, Mr Sykes," Mildred replied coolly. "How fortunate for you there's a market for both."

As they walked away, Mildred realised that the mystery deepened with each new revelation, the truth obscured by the same passionate intensity that made music soar. Somewhere in this tangle of artistic rivalry, secret arrangements, and hidden threats lay the key to Anton's death. Mildred was more determined than ever to find it.

12

Rain lashed against the windows of Mildred's study, transforming the glass into shimmering rivers of light and shadow. A fire crackled in the grate, its warm glow illuminating the array of papers spread across her desk. Outside, London had surrendered to the grip of autumn, but inside this sanctuary of thought, Mildred Ramsay was engaged in battle with a most peculiar enemy: a fragment of sheet music covered in Anton Lanyi's cramped Hungarian script.

She had been at it for hours, her normally tidy desk now resembling the aftermath of a particularly vigorous whirlwind. Reference books on music theory lay open beside Hungarian dictionaries borrowed from the London Library. Sheets of notepaper bore her careful transcriptions of the symbols and annotations, while a pot of tea had gone cold, forgotten in the intensity of her concentration.

"It's like the most infuriating crossword puzzle ever devised," she murmured to herself, rubbing her tired eyes.

The torn scrap from Anton's music had proven far more challenging than she had anticipated. What had initially appeared to be random jottings now revealed tantalising hints of deliberate patterning. Some annotations followed the staves of music, others clustered in the margins, and still others appeared in sequence, marked by tiny numbers that had almost escaped her notice.

Bea had departed an hour earlier, her patience for "silent staring at incomprehensible scribbles" thoroughly exhausted. Henry had looked in briefly, offered a bemused "Still at it, Millie?" and retreated to his club, recognising the particular set of his sister's jaw that signalled her complete absorption in a puzzle.

Left alone with the fragment, Mildred found herself cycling between frustration and exhilaration as small patterns emerged, only to dissolve again under closer scrutiny.

She reached for her notebook, flipping through pages of observations about the case. The cryptic note she'd found after Moretti's outburst. Volkov's bruised wrists and expensive wine. Nora's tonic bottle and broken dreams. Sylvia's whispered financial concerns. Each detail added complexity to a case that refused to resolve into a clear picture.

Returning to the sheet music, she traced a finger along a sequence of letters that had caught her attention earlier. Among the Hungarian words and musical annotations were scattered English initials: "O.K." appeared three times, each followed by numbers that might be dates or coordinates, or something else entirely.

"Otto Klein," she whispered, testing the name against the letters. The accompanist was perhaps the most enigmatic figure in Anton's circle. Quiet, efficient, always in the virtuoso's shadow. His calm demeanour during questioning had struck Mildred as either remarkable self-possession or the perfect mask for guilt.

But was she seeing connections where none existed? "O.K." could signify anything: "old key," "orchestra keeps," or simply the English expression of approval. Perhaps it wasn't even Anton's handwriting, but someone else's annotations added later.

She recalled Kent's frequent admonition: "Evidence first, theory second. Never the reverse."

Mildred sighed, acknowledging the wisdom in his caution. She had fallen into this trap before, constructing elegant theories that collapsed when confronted with an inconvenient fact. The coded notes remained stubbornly opaque, refusing to yield their secrets to her determined scrutiny.

Beside the sheet music lay the crumpled note she'd retrieved after Moretti's outburst: "If you speak of our arrangement to anyone, remember that you have far more to lose than I." Anton's elegant script carried a threat but against whom? Moretti's gambling debts provided obvious leverage, but the same message could have been directed at Otto, Sylvia, or even Volkov.

A sudden thought struck her. She pulled the sheet music closer, comparing the handwriting with the threatening note. Both featured the same distinctive loop on the capital 'I' and a slight rightward slant. But there was something else. A subtle difference in pressure, as if the musical annotations had been written with greater haste or tension.

Mildred reached for her magnifying glass, examining the "O.K." notations more carefully. The initials were indeed in Anton's hand, but the numbers that followed—"2/7," "4/5," "14/3"—had a mechanical precision that differed from his usual flowing script.

"Coordinates," she murmured, recalling her earlier

hypothesis. But coordinates to what? A map location? A page and line in a book?

Or perhaps...

She grabbed the Hungarian dictionary, flipping rapidly through its pages. What if the numbers referred not to locations but to words? The first number could indicate a page, the second a position on that page.

But which dictionary? Which edition? Without knowing what reference text Anton had used, the numbers remained meaningless.

Frustrated, Mildred pushed back from her desk and walked to the window, watching raindrops chase each other down the glass. The case was growing more complex with each discovery. Anton's death now seemed less like a simple murder born of jealousy or ambition and more like the removal of a key piece in a larger game.

What if the hollow violin case had indeed contained smuggled items? What if Anton's death was connected not to his music but to whatever illicit cargo he transported across European borders? And what if Otto Klein—the quiet, watchful accompanist—was more deeply involved than his placid exterior suggested?

A knock at the door interrupted her thoughts. Perkins, the elderly butler, entered with a silver tray bearing a fresh pot of tea and a small plate of biscuits.

"You missed dinner, my lady," he said, his voice carrying the gentle reproach of long service. "I took the liberty of bringing you something to sustain you in your... investigations."

Mildred smiled, gratitude washing over her. "Thank you, Perkins. I've lost track of time entirely."

"A common occurrence when you're on the scent, if I may say so." The old man's eyes twinkled, recalling the cases she had shared with him.

As he arranged the tea things on a side table, Perkins glanced at the sheet music. "Curious markings, those. Reminds me of the cipher books we used during my army days."

Mildred looked up sharply. "Cipher books?"

"Yes, my lady. Simple substitution ciphers, mostly. Each day had a different key." He tapped the numbers beside the 'O.K.' notations. "Those look like day and position indicators. First number tells you which day's cipher to use, second tells you where to start reading."

The observation, delivered with the casual certainty of experience, struck Mildred like a revelation. Of course—a cipher that changed regularly would require such indicators to be decipherable by the intended recipient.

"Perkins, you're brilliant," she exclaimed, causing the butler to flush with pleased embarrassment. "That would explain why some notations seem to follow no pattern. They're using different cipher keys."

"Happy to be of service, my lady." Perkins gave a small bow. "Though I should mention that Lady Beatrice telephoned earlier. She said to tell you she's arranged tea with Otto Klein tomorrow at Claridge's. Apparently, he was most eager to discuss Anton's musical legacy with an appreciative patron."

Mildred raised an eyebrow. Bea's talent for social manoeuvring never ceased to amaze her. "Did she indeed? How enterprising of her."

"She also mentioned something about bringing that Hungarian edition of Mozart you were inquiring after."

Perkins' face remained impassive, but his eyes held the knowing look of one long accustomed to the unspoken communications between the two friends.

"Thank you, Perkins. Please tell her I'll be delighted to join them."

After the butler withdrew, Mildred returned to her desk with fresh purpose. If the numbers did indicate cipher keys, she might need the actual code book to decipher Anton's notes. But even without it, certain patterns might emerge under careful analysis.

She began grouping the annotations by their numerical indicators, searching for commonalities. The "O.K." notations all appeared with different numbers, suggesting they might represent different instructions or locations. If Otto Klein was indeed involved, these could be records of transactions or meeting points.

Yet as she worked, a nagging doubt persisted. Was she allowing her suspicion of Otto to colour her interpretation of the evidence? The initials could refer to anything or anyone. Confirmation bias was the amateur detective's greatest pitfall, leading one to see only what one expected to find.

"Follow the evidence, not your suppositions," she reminded herself, echoing Kent's favourite admonition.

With renewed discipline, she forced herself to consider alternative explanations. Perhaps "O.K." referred not to Otto Klein but to a location—Oslo Kringsjå, or Oxford Kinema, or Old Kent Road. Perhaps it was a code phrase with no relation to initials at all. Perhaps, most simply, it meant exactly what it appeared to mean: "okay," a confirmation that something had been done or received.

The teacup beside her had grown cold again when she noticed another pattern. The numbers following "O.K."

corresponded to dates in the previous months—February 7th, April 5th, and most recently, October 14th. If these were dates rather than cipher keys, they might indicate a regular schedule of some kind.

Mildred flipped through her calendar, checking whether these dates coincided with Anton's known concert performances. To her surprise, none matched his public appearances. Whatever these dates referred to, it wasn't his official musical engagements.

She made a careful note of this discovery, adding it to her growing catalogue of questions. Tomorrow's meeting with Otto Klein might provide an opportunity to observe his reactions to casual mentions of these dates or locations. If he was indeed the "O.K." in Anton's notes, any flicker of recognition might betray him.

But caution was essential. If Otto was involved in Anton's death, he was clearly capable of careful planning and discretion. The poisoned tonic bottle, if that was indeed the murder weapon, had required intimate knowledge of Anton's routine and access to his personal belongings. As accompanist, Otto had both.

Yet the same could be said for Moretti, who conducted the performance, or Sylvia, who frequented the backstage area as Anton's patroness. Even Nora, despite her apparent innocence, had backstage access as the understudy violinist.

"Don't leap to conclusions," Mildred murmured, gathering the scattered papers into a more organised arrangement. "Observe first, deduce second."

She carefully tucked the sheet music fragment and her notes into a leather portfolio, securing it with a ribbon. Tomorrow's tea at Claridge's would be an opportunity for subtle observation, not confrontation. She would watch Otto's hands, listen to his choice of words, note any nervousness when certain topics arose.

The rain had stopped, leaving the windows streaked with glistening trails. Beyond the glass, London slumbered under a canopy of stars partly obscured by lingering clouds. Somewhere in that city, a killer walked free, perhaps believing themselves safe from discovery.

As Mildred prepared for bed, her mind circled back to the cipher-like notations in Anton's music. If they did indeed record some secret arrangement—smuggling, perhaps, or payments, or meetings—they might provide the key to his murder. But without the cipher key, they remained tantalisingly out of reach.

The memory of Perkins' casual observation lingered. Simple substitution ciphers, with different keys for different days. A system designed for communication between those who shared a secret language. Anton and his accomplice, or perhaps his killer, had communicated through these coded notes, leaving a trail that Mildred was now struggling to follow.

She drifted off to sleep with fragments of the code dancing behind her eyelids. In her dreams, the musical notations transformed into a winding path through a labyrinth, each turn marked with cryptic signposts bearing the initials "O.K." At the centre waited a shadowy figure, face obscured, a violin case held protectively in gloved hands.

Tomorrow, she would come face to face with Otto Klein, the quiet accompanist who had stood in Anton's shadow for years. Would she see in his eyes the truth behind those enigmatic initials? Or would she find herself following yet another false trail in the increasingly complex mystery of the vanishing violinist?

The answer, like the code itself, remained just beyond her grasp—a puzzle waiting for the final piece that would bring everything into focus.

13

The morning dawned with crisp autumn sunshine, a deceptive brightness that did little to warm the bite in the air. Mildred adjusted her hat as she stepped out of the cab onto Brook Street, her leather portfolio tucked securely under her arm. Inside lay her carefully organised notes on Anton's mysterious coded music, including the peculiar "O.K." annotations she'd spent half the night analysing.

Claridge's stood before her, its elegant façade a monument to discretion and luxury. As she approached the entrance, Mildred found herself glancing over her shoulder, unable to shake the sensation that she was being observed. A man in a dark overcoat lingered near a newspaper stand across the street, his face hidden behind the morning edition of The Times. When she paused, he turned slightly away, the gesture too deliberate to be coincidental.

Mildred continued toward the hotel, her pace measured but alert. As she passed a polished shop window, she used its reflection to confirm her suspicion: the man had folded his newspaper and begun to follow at a cautious distance.

The doorman greeted her with a respectful nod, swinging open the heavy door with practised grace. Inside, the hotel's hushed opulence enveloped her like a velvet cloak. Crystal chandeliers cast their gentle light over the immaculate marble floors, while discreet staff moved like shadows among the potted palms and tasteful furnishings.

Mildred paused in the lobby, ostensibly adjusting her gloves while watching the entrance in a conveniently placed mirror. A full minute passed, then two. The man who had been following her did not enter. Either he had abandoned his pursuit or, more likely, was content to wait outside until she emerged.

"Lady Mildred!" Bea's cheerful voice carried across the lobby, drawing several politely disapproving glances from the other guests. She was seated in the far corner of the tea room, waving enthusiastically. Beside her sat a slender man in his forties, immaculately dressed in a charcoal suit that spoke of careful attention to appearance despite limited means.

Otto Klein.

As Mildred approached, she was surprised to find both Bea and Otto laughing together like old friends, his typically reserved demeanour noticeably softened. Bea had a talent for disarming even the most guarded personalities, but the ease between them was unexpected.

"Darling, you must hear what Mr Klein was just telling me about the time Anton tried to conduct an orchestra in Vienna while suffering from influenza," Bea exclaimed as Mildred joined them. "Apparently he sneezed so violently during the crescendo that his baton went flying into the double bass!"

Otto's smile lingered, transforming his usually watchful face into something warmer, more human. "Anton insisted we never speak of it again, but he couldn't help laughing whenever he saw that particular bassist thereafter."

Mildred settled into her chair, studying the accompanist with fresh interest. "It sounds as though you knew him quite well, Mr Klein."

"Please, call me Otto," he replied, his English nearly perfect but for the slight Central European lilt that softened his consonants. "And yes, I knew Anton for nearly fifteen years. Since Budapest, before the war."

A waiter appeared with fresh tea and an assortment of delicate pastries. As he poured, Otto's gaze seemed to drift to some distant memory, his long fingers absently tracing the edge of his saucer.

"How did you meet?" Mildred asked, accepting her cup with a murmured thanks.

Otto's expression warmed with recollection. "At the Academy of Music in Budapest. I was a scholarship student, the son of a clockmaker with delusions of artistic greatness. Anton was already something of a prodigy but struggling with theory classes." His smile deepened. "He could play like an angel but couldn't tell you which key he was in. I offered to help him prepare for examinations; in return, he taught me to feel the music beyond the notes."

"A fair exchange," Mildred observed.

"More than fair," Otto replied. "I was painfully shy, too afraid of mistakes to play with true passion. Anton would say, 'Otto, the notes are just the skeleton. You must give them flesh, blood, breath!'" His impression of Anton's intensity was startlingly accurate. "He made me brave enough to perform."

Bea sighed romantically. "How wonderful to have such a

friendship. Though I imagine there were difficult moments too?"

Otto nodded, his smile fading slightly. "When the war came, everything changed. Hungary was in chaos afterward. Many of us lost everything—homes, family, certainty. Anton helped me escape to Vienna, found me work in the opera house there. Later, when he secured his first major tour, he insisted I accompany him." His voice softened. "He said, 'We refugees must stick together, yes? Music is our only true country now.'"

Mildred watched him carefully as he spoke, noting the genuine emotion that flickered across his features. Either Otto Klein was indeed mourning a dear friend, or he was a performer of extraordinary skill.

"He sounds like a loyal friend," she said. "It must have been devastating to lose him so suddenly."

Something complicated passed behind Otto's eyes—grief, certainly, but perhaps something else too. Guilt? Fear? It was gone before she could be certain.

"Anton had a great heart," Otto replied after a moment. "Especially for his people—Hungarians, musicians, anyone displaced by the war. He used his success to help others whenever he could."

"How admirable," Mildred said, deliberately casual as she reached for a pastry. "Did that include financial assistance? I understand musicians can struggle, even successful ones."

Otto hesitated briefly. "Anton was generous, yes. Though his patroness, Mrs Harcourt, sometimes objected to what she called his 'charitable impulses.' She preferred he focus on his career."

"Sylvia does seem rather possessive of her artists," Bea interjected. "I heard she nearly had a dreadful tantrum when Anton considered playing for Lady Ivy's musical evening instead of her charity gala last spring."

Otto's smile turned wry. "Anton enjoyed playing patrons against each other. He would say, 'Let them compete for the privilege of our art, Otto. It is the only power we have in their world.'"

"Was that why he was considering breaking his contract with Sylvia?" Mildred asked, recalling the whispered conversation she'd overheard at the concert.

Again, that slight hesitation. "Anton was... restless lately. He spoke of returning to Hungary, of using his influence to help rebuild musical institutions there."

"A noble ambition," Mildred said, "though perhaps financially challenging?"

Otto met her gaze directly. "Anton never worried about money. He believed true artists would always find patrons or manage without them."

Something in his tone suggested there was more to this philosophy than artistic idealism. Mildred thought of the coded notes, the hollow violin case, the rumours of valuables transported across borders. Had Anton's financial confidence stemmed from activities beyond his concert performances?

Bea, sensing the subtle tension, steered the conversation toward lighter topics—amusing backstage anecdotes, the eccentricities of various conductors, Otto's own musical education. Throughout, Otto remained charming and forthcoming, his initial reserve all but vanished in the warmth of shared recollections.

As their meeting drew to a close, Mildred finally broached the subject that had occupied her thoughts. "I understand you often prepared Anton's tonic before performances. Was that part of your routine together?"

If the question surprised him, Otto didn't show it. "Yes, a small superstition. He was particular about taking it exactly five minutes before walking on stage—not four, not six. He claimed it steadied his hands."

"The tonic that was found beside him after his collapse," Mildred ventured. "Was it the same preparation he always used?"

Otto's expression clouded. "I believe so. A Hungarian remedy his mother had made for him since childhood. He had it specially imported."

"And you prepared it for him that night?"

His gaze met hers, unwavering. "I did. Just as I had done hundreds of times before."

The implied question hung in the air between them: If the tonic had been poisoned, was Otto admitting to being the last person to handle it? Or was he confident in his innocence, perhaps knowing the poison had been administered in some other way?

"How dreadful for you," Bea said softly, patting his hand. "To think that something you did as an act of friendship might be connected to his death."

Otto looked down at her hand on his, genuine emotion surfacing in his eyes. "I have asked myself many times if I could have prevented it somehow. If I missed something that night, some small detail..." He trailed off, then squared his shoulders with visible effort. "But I must believe that whoever did this will be found. Anton deserves justice."

As they prepared to leave, Otto retrieved a small leather-bound volume from his pocket. "Lady Mildred, I understand you have an interest in music. This was Anton's marked copy. Perhaps it will comfort you to see his hand on the page."

Mildred accepted the book with carefully concealed surprise. "This is most generous, Mr Klein. Are you certain you wish to part with it?"

He smiled sadly. "Anton would have wanted it in the hands of someone who values both music and truth. Besides, I have many other keepsakes of our years together."

Outside Claridge's, as they bid Otto farewell, Bea turned to Mildred with bright eyes. "Well? What did you think of our melancholy pianist? Isn't he perfectly tragic and romantic?"

Mildred watched Otto's retreating figure, noting how his shoulders seemed to tense once more as he rejoined the bustling street. "He's certainly compelling. The question is whether we witnessed genuine grief or a masterful performance."

"You don't believe his tender reminiscences?" Bea looked disappointed.

"I believe he cared for Anton," Mildred replied thoughtfully. "But caring for someone doesn't preclude harming them, especially if other pressures are involved."

As they walked toward Oxford Street, Mildred casually scanned the passing faces, searching for the man who had followed her earlier. There was no sign of him, though the sensation of being observed persisted like a phantom touch between her shoulder blades.

"He gave you Anton's music book," Bea pointed out. "That seems a gesture of trust, doesn't it?"

"Or a calculated risk," Mildred mused. "Perhaps he knows what I'm looking for and wants to appear cooperative. Or perhaps the book contains something he wants me to find."

Bea's eyes widened with excitement. "A clue! Oh, how thrilling. Shall we examine it over tea at Fortnum's?"

But Mildred's attention had shifted to a reflection in a shop window—a glimpse of a familiar dark overcoat several yards behind them. "Actually, Bea," she said quietly, "I think we're being followed. Let's take a cab directly home instead."

As they hailed a cab, Mildred carefully tucked the music book into her portfolio alongside her notes. Otto Klein had presented himself as a loyal friend mourning a tragic loss. His stories rang with emotional truth, his grief seemed palpable, his affection for Anton appeared genuine.

Yet Mildred couldn't dismiss the careful calculation she'd glimpsed beneath his reminiscences. Otto had admitted to handling the tonic bottle but offered no explanation for how poison might have entered it. He had acknowledged Anton's restlessness and desire to break free from certain arrangements but provided no details about what those arrangements might have entailed.

Most intriguing of all, he had freely given her a book of Anton's personal annotations, the very sort of document she had been attempting to decipher.

Was it possible that Otto Klein had just handed her the key to unravelling Anton's death? Or was he deliberately leading her down a carefully constructed false trail?

As their cab pulled away from the kerb, Mildred caught one last glimpse of the man in the overcoat. He stood watching their departure, his face finally visible for a brief moment before he turned away.

It was not, as she had half-expected, Otto Klein ensuring she had left Claridge's. Nor was it Inspector Kent keeping tabs on her unofficial investigation.

The face was unfamiliar, foreign, with the hard, assessing gaze of someone accustomed to remaining unnoticed while taking careful measure of others.

Mildred settled back against the seat, her mind racing. The game, it seemed, had more players than she had anticipated. And someone—someone beyond the immediate circle of suspects—was taking a keen interest in her pursuit of Anton Lanyi's killer.

14

"Absolutely not," declared Henry, folding his newspaper with a decisive snap. "I've indulged enough of your detective fancies, Mildred. Prowling around questionable establishments on the riverside is where I draw the line."

Mildred regarded her brother with the patient expression she reserved for particularly stubborn patients during her nursing days. The morning light filtering through the breakfast room windows cast a gentle glow on the remains of their meal—toast crusts, marmalade jar, Henry's half-empty teacup. She had waited until he was nearly finished before broaching the subject of the Magyar Kávéház, a café tucked beneath the railway arches near the Thames.

"It's hardly questionable, Henry," she replied mildly. "It's simply a gathering place for Hungarian and Austrian musicians. Quite respectable, if somewhat bohemian."

"Bohemian!" Henry's moustache twitched with disapproval. "Precisely my point. Not a suitable establishment for a lady of your standing."

Beatrice, who had arrived unannounced for breakfast as was her custom three days a week, chose this moment to intervene. "Oh, but Henry, don't you see? That's exactly why Mildred needs you as an escort. Who better to protect her virtue than her stalwart brother?"

Henry's expression wavered between irritation at the manipulation and pride at the description. "I hardly think—"

"Besides," Bea continued, helping herself to another slice of toast, "I've heard their strudel is divine. Haven't you always said that Austrian pastry is superior to French?"

This was a masterstroke, appealing to Henry's well-known culinary opinions. He frowned, torn between his principles and his sweet tooth.

Mildred pressed her advantage. "It would only be for an hour or so this afternoon. I've heard that several of Anton's former colleagues frequent the place. They might provide insights that more... official channels have missed."

"By 'official channels,' I assume you mean Inspector Kent," Henry said dryly. "Whom you've been deliberately avoiding since your disagreement."

"Not avoiding," Mildred corrected. "Simply pursuing alternative avenues of inquiry."

"Well, I suppose someone must keep an eye on you two," Henry sighed, his capitulation evident. "But we shall leave at the first sign of anything untoward. And no engaging with suspicious characters!"

Bea clapped her hands in delight. "Splendid! I shall wear my new cloche hat. It has just the right amount of bohemian flair without being scandalous."

"I thought you had a luncheon engagement with Lady Westmorland today," Mildred remarked, raising an eyebrow.

Bea's enthusiasm dimmed momentarily. "Oh bother, so I do. Well, you must tell me absolutely everything. Especially about the strudel."

By three o'clock that afternoon, Mildred and Henry were making their way along the narrow street that ran parallel to the Thames. The sky had cleared after a morning shower, and weak autumn sunshine glinted off the river. The arches that supported the railway bridge housed a variety of small businesses—a cobbler, a bookbinder, and, at the far end, the café.

The Magyar Kávéház announced itself with a modest sign and a red geranium in the window. Despite its humble exterior, the café was surprisingly warm and inviting inside. Small tables covered with embroidered cloths filled the space, while an upright piano stood in one corner. The walls were decorated with faded photographs of Budapest and Vienna, interspersed with framed concert programmes from various European venues.

The clientele was an eclectic mix: elderly men playing chess, young artists sketching in notebooks, and musicians identifiable by the instrument cases propped beside their chairs. Conversations in Hungarian, German, and accented English created a gentle babble that rose and fell like distant music.

A stout woman in her fifties approached them, wiping her hands on her apron. "Welcome, welcome," she said, her English precise but heavily accented. "Table for two? By window, yes?"

Henry, having apparently decided to embrace the adventure, nodded with unexpected graciousness. "That would be splendid, thank you."

As they settled at a small table overlooking the street, Mildred surveyed the room with practiced casualness. Near the piano, three men were engaged in animated conversation, their gestures suggesting a heated debate about music or politics—or perhaps both, given the passion evident in their expressions.

"The strudel, Henry," she murmured. "You must try it. I hear it's authentic Viennese."

Taking the hint, Henry summoned the proprietress and ordered coffee and apple strudel for them both. As she bustled away, Mildred shifted her chair slightly, angling herself to better overhear the nearby conversations without appearing to eavesdrop.

"...still cannot believe it," one of the men near the piano was saying, his accent thick with emotion. "Anton, of all people. So careful, always so careful."

"That is the risk, yes?" replied his companion, a gaunt man with thinning grey hair. "The higher you climb, the further to fall. And with such valuable cargo..."

Mildred kept her gaze fixed on the menu card, though she had already decided on her order. Her pulse quickened at the mention of Anton's name and the tantalising reference to "valuable cargo."

"Remind me again how you learned of this establishment?" Henry asked, oblivious to the significant conversation nearby.

"Lady Ivy mentioned it," Mildred replied, lowering her voice to encourage Henry to do the same. "She patronises several émigré musicians and said they speak highly of this place."

The proprietress returned with their coffee, the rich aroma momentarily distracting Mildred from her eavesdropping. When she tuned back into the conversation, the men had lowered their voices, forcing her to strain to catch their words.

"...third time this year," the gaunt man was saying. "The emeralds from Warsaw, the documents from Prague, and now this. They say his violin case had a compartment so cleverly made even the customs men never found it."

Mildred nearly spilled her coffee. Here, finally, was confirmation of her theory about Anton's hollow violin case. Not from official channels or reluctant witnesses, but from the casual conversation of those who had known him and his activities.

"Ssh, not so loud," cautioned the third man, glancing nervously around the café. "The police still investigate. And remember what happened to Volkov when he spoke too freely."

"Ah, poor Volkov," nodded the first man. "Bruises like plums on his wrists. A warning, yes? To keep silent about the arrangements."

Mildred's mind raced. Volkov's bruises, which he had claimed came from a workshop accident, were actually the result of intimidation. But by whom? And what "arrangements" was he being warned to keep silent about?

"They say the accompanist has taken leave," the gaunt man added, stirring his coffee thoughtfully. "Gone back to Vienna, perhaps. Or further east."

"Clever man," grunted his companion. "Better to be elsewhere than face questions about certain... activities."

This new piece of information intrigued Mildred. Otto had been at Claridge's just days ago, apparently mourning his friend's death and generous enough to give her Anton's annotated Mozart scores. Had he departed since then? And was his departure related to these 'activities' the men mentioned?

"Moretti is beside himself," the gaunt man continued. "First Anton steals his cadenza, then dies in his concert, now the investigation threatens his reputation. They say he's drinking heavily."

"And that patroness, the English widow," added the third man. "She's selling paintings from her collection. Desperate for funds, they say."

Mildred listened intently as the conversation drifted from one suspect to another, each mentioned with the same mix of speculation and insider knowledge. Sylvia's financial troubles, Moretti's artistic grievances, even Nora's thwarted ambitions—all were discussed with the casual certainty of those adjacent to, but not directly involved in, the drama.

The arrival of their strudel interrupted her thoughts. The pastry was indeed magnificent; layers of paper-thin dough filled with spiced apples and dusted with powdered sugar. Henry's expression of surprised delight suggested Bea's strategy had been entirely successful.

"I must say, Mildred, your unconventional excursions occasionally yield delightful results," he admitted, cutting into the strudel with evident appreciation.

Mildred smiled, though her mind remained focused on the fragments of conversation she had overheard. "I'm glad you approve, Henry. Sometimes the most valuable discoveries come from unexpected places."

As they enjoyed their pastry, the men at the piano table rose to leave, still conversing in low tones. Mildred watched them from the corner of her eye, noting how they nodded respectfully to the proprietress before departing. One of them, the gaunt man with thinning hair, paused to retrieve a violin case from beside his chair, handling it with the care of a dedicated musician.

A violin case, much like Anton's. Perhaps with its own secrets hidden within.

When they had gone, Mildred sipped her coffee thoughtfully. The puzzle was starting to take a clearer shape. Anton Lanyi had been using his position as a celebrated violinist to transport valuable items across European borders—emeralds, documents, perhaps other precious cargo. The hollow compartment in his violin case, which Volkov had created at Anton's request, had served as the perfect hiding place, beyond the scrutiny of customs officials dazzled by his celebrity.

But who else was involved in this smuggling operation? The men had mentioned several names in connection with Anton's activities—Volkov, certainly, who had crafted the secret compartment. Otto, as his constant companion, must have been aware, if not actively involved. Sylvia, whose financial troubles might have driven her to participate or profit. Even Moretti, whose artistic outrage might mask deeper entanglements.

"You're very quiet, Mildred," Henry observed, interrupting her thoughts. "Not that I'm complaining, mind you, but it usually means you're piecing together something troublesome."

Mildred smiled faintly. "Just enjoying the ambiance, Henry. And the excellent strudel."

He regarded her sceptically. "I've known you since you were in leading strings, Millie. That's your 'puzzle-solving' expression. What have you discovered?"

She hesitated, weighing how much to share. Henry's protective instincts, while well-intentioned, sometimes limited her freedom to investigate. Yet his practical perspective often helped clarify her thinking.

"I believe Anton Lanyi was involved in smuggling valuable items across borders," she said finally. "Using his violin case to conceal them during his concert tours."

Henry's eyebrows shot up. "Good Lord. That sounds rather more serious than a simple murder."

"Murder is never simple, Henry," Mildred replied. "But you're right—this suggests a network of connections beyond the immediate circle of suspects. And potentially a more complex motive than personal jealousy or artistic rivalry."

"You should take this to Inspector Kent," Henry advised, lowering his voice. "International smuggling is hardly a matter for amateur investigation, no matter how clever the amateur."

Mildred nodded, though inwardly she knew she would pursue her own inquiries further before approaching Kent. His dismissive response to her earlier theory about the violin case still rankled, and she wanted more concrete evidence before facing his scepticism again.

As they prepared to leave, Mildred paused to study the framed concert programmes on the wall. One from Vienna caught her eye—a performance at the Musikverein featuring Anton Lanyi as soloist, with Otto Klein as accompanist. The date at the top: March 14th, 1924.

She scanned the other programmes, noting similar performances in Warsaw and Prague. The pattern was becoming clear: Anton's concert tours had taken him to precisely the cities mentioned by the gaunt man in connection with smuggled items—emeralds from Warsaw, documents from Prague, something unspecified from Vienna.

The hollow violin case had indeed held more than music; it had concealed valuables transported across borders under the guise of cultural exchange. But who had killed Anton, and why? Was it a fellow conspirator fearing exposure? Someone cheated out of their share? Or perhaps an outsider who had discovered the smuggling operation and sought to end it?

As she and Henry departed the café, Mildred's mind was racing with implications. Anton's death wasn't merely the result of artistic jealousy or personal revenge. It was connected to a sophisticated smuggling operation that had gone awry. The question now was which of the suspects in their growing circle had the most to gain, or lose, from Anton's sudden silencing.

Was it Sylvia, desperate to escape financial ruin? Moretti, whose artistic outrage might conceal deeper involvement? Volkov, intimidated into compliance but perhaps driven to eliminate the source of his fear? Otto, whose quiet competence might mask a calculating mind? Or someone else entirely, a player in the shadows whose role had yet to emerge?

"You're plotting something, Millie," Henry said as they walked back toward the main road to hail a cab. "I can see it in your eyes."

"Not plotting, Henry," she replied with a small smile. "Simply following the notes where they lead."

The case was expanding beyond the confines of the Royal Albert Hall, beyond the circle of musicians and patrons who had witnessed Anton's collapse. It now stretched across Europe, involving emeralds and documents, secret compartments and coded messages—a symphony of intrigue where each suspect might play a crucial part, and where the final, revealing chord had yet to sound.

15

The evening descended upon London like a theatre curtain, bringing with it a fog that transformed familiar streets into mysterious, shrouded corridors. Gaslights glowed in diffused halos, their warmth barely penetrating the damp grey veil that wrapped the city in silence. Mildred and Beatrice made their way carefully along the embankment, their footsteps muffled against the wet cobblestones.

"I still think we should have brought Henry," Bea whispered, clutching her parasol like a weapon. Despite the lack of rain, she had insisted on bringing it. "For protection, darling. One never knows when one might need to fend off nefarious characters."

"Henry would have insisted we return home at the first sign of fog," Mildred replied, her voice low. "Besides, we're merely following up on a perfectly innocent lead."

The "perfectly innocent lead" in question had come from one of Lady Ivy's more reliable gossips: a small music shop near the Thames had received an after-hours visitor who matched the description of someone in Anton's circle. Nothing suspicious about a musician visiting such an establishment, except that he had done so with evident secrecy.

"Tell me again why we're skulking about in this dreadful soup?" Bea asked, her fashionable shoes already damp from the mist-slicked pavement.

"Because I believe this shop might hold answers about Anton's affairs," Mildred explained patiently. "Lady Ivy's source mentioned seeing someone hurrying away with a package the size of a music folio."

"Hardly damning evidence," Bea sighed dramatically. "Half of London carries music folios. Though I suppose one can't expect murderers to advertise themselves with signs and banners."

Mildred smiled despite herself. Bea's frivolity often disguised a sharper mind than many gave her credit for. "Precisely. And if this shop is indeed connected to Anton in some way, it may help us understand what made him a target."

They turned down a narrow side street where the fog seemed to gather more thickly, clinging to the buildings like spectral drapery. The music shop stood midway along the row, its darkened window displaying an assortment of tuning forks, metronomes, and brass instruments that caught occasional glints from the distant street lamps.

"It's closed," Bea observed unnecessarily, peering through the grimy glass.

"Yes, but there's a light at the back." Mildred gestured toward a faint yellow glow visible through the shop's depths. "Someone's working late."

They moved toward the alley that ran alongside the building, seeking a rear entrance. The passage was narrow and slick with moisture, forcing them to proceed in single file. Bea clutched Mildred's coat with one hand, her parasol at the ready in the other.

"If we're murdered in this horrid little alley," she whispered, "I shall be very cross with you, Mildred Ramsay."

"Duly noted," Mildred replied, suppressing a chuckle. "Though I suspect we're more likely to catch cold than meet with violence."

No sooner had the words left her mouth than a door at the rear of the shop burst open, spilling yellow light into the fog. A figure emerged, tall, masculine, moving with urgent purpose. Before either woman could react, he had plunged into the narrow alley, colliding with them in his haste.

Mildred found herself pressed against the damp brick wall as the man pushed past, his shoulder knocking her sideways. Bea, with the surprising reflexes that occasionally emerged from her otherwise languid demeanour, let out an indignant squawk and swung her parasol in a wide arc.

"Unhand us, you brute!" she cried, connecting solidly with the man's shoulder.

There was a grunt of pain, a muttered oath in what sounded like German or perhaps Hungarian, and then the figure was shoving past them, disappearing into the swirling fog with remarkable speed for someone who had just been assaulted by an outraged society lady wielding silk and whalebone.

"Well!" Bea exclaimed, straightening her hat, which had been knocked askew in the encounter. "Did you see that? He nearly flattened us! And not so much as an 'excuse me'!"

Mildred, however, was not listening. She was bent low, examining something that glinted on the wet cobblestones where the man had dropped it in his hasty retreat. It was a small metal instrument, shaped like an elongated key with an unusual square head.

"A piano-tuner's key," she murmured, turning it over in her gloved hand. "Used to adjust the tension of the strings."

"How fascinating," Bea replied, in a tone suggesting it was anything but. "Meanwhile, we've just been accosted by a fleeing criminal who may well return with reinforcements."

"He won't," Mildred said with quiet certainty, still studying the key. "He was as surprised by our presence as we were by his. That wasn't a planned escape; it was a panicked flight."

She straightened, slipping the key into her coat pocket. As she did so, she became aware of a lingering scent in the damp air, subtle but distinctive, the resinous sweetness of violin rosin mixed with the sharper notes of linseed oil and varnish. The same fragrance she had noticed around Anton on the night of the concert, and later in Volkov's workshop.

"Did you notice his scent?" she asked Bea, who was still huffing indignantly and adjusting her dishevelled attire.

"I was rather too occupied with avoiding being trampled to catalogue his cologne," Bea replied tartly. "Though I did notice he seemed unconcerned with the niceties of personal hygiene."

"Not that," Mildred shook her head. "Rosin. The substance violinists use on their bows. And linseed oil, used for treating wooden instruments."

Bea's irritation faded, replaced by growing interest. "You think he might be connected to the musical world? Perhaps someone from Anton's circle?"

"It's possible," Mildred said thoughtfully, moving toward the now-closed door. "The scent was quite strong, as if he works closely with instruments."

The door was firmly shut, a heavy padlock now visible in the dim light. Whatever the fleeing man had been doing inside the shop, he had taken care to secure it before his departure.

Mildred examined the door frame carefully, noting a fresh scratch in the paint near the lock. "Someone picked this lock recently," she observed. "Not a regular visitor with a key."

"A burglar?" Bea suggested, peering over Mildred's shoulder.

"Perhaps. Or someone searching for something specific." Mildred stepped back, surveying the narrow windows that lined the upper portion of the building. All were dark and securely shuttered.

"What do we do now?" Bea asked, clutching her parasol more tightly as a particularly thick bank of fog rolled through the alley. "Break in ourselves? That seems rather more criminal than our usual activities."

"No," Mildred replied decisively. "We'll come back during regular hours. But first, I'd like to examine this key more carefully."

As they made their way back to the main street, Mildred couldn't shake the feeling that they had stumbled onto something significant. The fleeing figure, the piano-tuner's key, the scent of rosin and linseed oil, all connected to the world of music in which Anton had moved. But what had the man been searching for in the shop? And why had he fled in such panic?

"Do you think it could have been someone we know?" Bea asked as they emerged onto a better-lit thoroughfare.

"Possible," Mildred conceded. "Though I couldn't see his face clearly in this fog."

"What about his height? His build? Anything distinctive?"

Mildred considered this as they hailed a cab. "Tall, certainly. Broad-shouldered. The oath sounded Central European rather than English or Italian."

"That narrows it down somewhat," Bea mused as the cab arrived. "Though half the musicians in London seem to be from Budapest or Vienna these days."

They climbed into the cab gratefully, giving Mildred's address to the driver. As they settled onto the worn leather seats, Mildred turned the piano-tuner's key over in her gloved fingers. It was heavier than it looked, the metal cool against her skin even through the fabric of her gloves.

"It's an unusual design," she noted, studying the square head more closely. "Most piano-tuner's keys have a simple socket end."

Bea leaned closer, suddenly interested. "It looks almost like it could be hollow. See how the shaft widens slightly before the handle?"

Mildred examined the key with renewed attention. Bea was right. There was a subtle flare in the metal shaft just before it met the wooden handle, almost as if the two parts were separate pieces fitted together.

"Bea, you're brilliant," she murmured, carefully twisting the wooden handle. It resisted at first, then gave way with a soft click, rotating counter-clockwise to reveal a threaded join.

"Oh my," Bea breathed, eyes widening. "It is hollow! What a clever hiding place. Though rather small for smuggling anything valuable, I should think."

Mildred gently unscrewed the handle from the metal shaft, revealing a tiny cavity within. It was empty now, but clearly designed to conceal something small. A gem, perhaps, or a folded document.

"Not so small if what you're hiding is precious enough," Mildred replied, thinking of the conversation she had overheard at the émigré café.

The cab rattled through the foggy streets, carrying them back to the familiar comfort of Mayfair. But Mildred's thoughts remained in that dimly lit alley, with the fleeing figure whose identity remained concealed by the fog. Whoever he was, he had been searching for something specific in that music shop, something important enough to risk breaking in after hours.

And whatever it was, it connected somehow to the piano-tuner's key now resting in her palm, with its clever hidden compartment designed for secrets.

As they approached her home, Mildred carefully reassembled the key, tucking it securely into her reticule. Tomorrow, she would visit the music shop during business hours, perhaps discover who owned it and what connection it might have to Anton's circle. For now, she had a new piece to add to the puzzle, a tangible link to the shadowy world Anton had inhabited.

"Penny for your thoughts?" Bea asked as the cab slowed to a halt.

Mildred smiled faintly. "I was just wondering who our fleeing friend might be. And what he hoped to find in that shop."

"We may never know," Bea sighed dramatically. "Though I do hope we encounter him again. My parasol and I have unfinished business."

As they stepped down from the cab into the swirling London fog, Mildred couldn't help glancing back the way they had come. Somewhere in this vast city, a man with the scent of rosin on his clothes was nursing a bruised shoulder and, perhaps, a guilty conscience. Whether he was killer or accomplice, witness or innocent bystander, remained to be seen.

But one thing was certain. The hollow key in her reticule had been designed for secrecy. And in Mildred's experience, secrets were seldom innocent in the shadow of murder.

16

Morning arrived with a damp chill that seeped beneath doors and whistled through window frames. Mildred sat at her writing desk, examining the piano-tuner's key by daylight. Its hollow centre remained the most intriguing aspect—a perfect hiding place for something small but precious. She had just begun to make notes when Perkins appeared at her study door, his customary composure noticeably disturbed.

"Inspector Kent is here to see you, my lady. He seems rather... urgent."

Mildred glanced up, surprised. "This early? Show him in, please."

She hastily tucked the key into her desk drawer as Kent strode into the room. His usual measured calm had given way to a barely contained energy that suggested significant developments.

"Lady Mildred," he began without preamble, "I thought you should hear this directly from me. We've arrested Nora Bellamy for the murder of Anton Lanyi."

Mildred stared at him in disbelief. "Nora? Surely not."

"I'm afraid the evidence is quite compelling." Kent removed his hat, revealing hair slightly dishevelled, as if he had been running his hands through it in frustration. "A search of her rooms revealed a vial of cyanide compound hidden in her violin case. Chemical analysis confirms it matches the poison found in Anton's system."

"That's impossible," Mildred protested. "When I spoke with her, she was frightened, yes, but not guilty."

"Fear and guilt often present similar symptoms, Lady Mildred. Particularly in those unaccustomed to crime."

His tone held that familiar note of professional certainty that had irked her during previous investigations. Mildred rose from her chair, collecting her coat and hat from the stand by the door.

"Where is she being held?"

Kent sighed, having clearly anticipated this reaction. "At Scotland Yard for questioning. But I didn't come to invite your participation in the interrogation."

"No, I imagine you didn't," Mildred replied with a thin smile. "Yet here we are. Shall we take your police car, or would you prefer a cab?"

For a moment, it seemed Kent might refuse, but experience had long since taught him the futility of opposing Mildred when her mind was set. "The car is waiting outside," he conceded. "Though I must warn you, this is not like our previous... collaborations. The evidence is straightforward."

"Too straightforward, perhaps," Mildred murmured, but she allowed Kent to escort her outside.

The drive to Scotland Yard passed in tense silence, broken only by Kent's brief explanations of the morning's events. A tip from an anonymous caller had prompted the search of Nora's lodgings. The vial had been found wrapped in sheet music and tucked into a hidden pocket of her violin case, along with several newspaper clippings about Anton's death.

"And did Nora have an explanation for these items?" Mildred inquired.

"She claims they were planted," Kent replied, his tone neutral but faintly sceptical. "A convenient defence, but hardly original."

"Or perhaps the truth," Mildred countered. "You must admit, Inspector, that Nora seems an unlikely poisoner. She had ambition, certainly, but limited opportunity and questionable motive."

"Limited opportunity?" Kent raised an eyebrow. "She was backstage throughout the evening, with access to Anton's dressing room. As for motive, we have multiple witnesses who confirm that Anton had promised her a featured solo, only to withdraw it days before the concert."

"A professional disappointment, yes. Hardly grounds for murder."

"You'd be surprised what injured pride can drive people to do," Kent replied grimly. "Particularly when combined with thwarted ambition and public humiliation."

They arrived at Scotland Yard to find a small crowd of journalists already gathered outside, alerted by some internal leak to the arrest of a suspect in the sensational Lanyi case. Kent ushered Mildred through a side entrance, sparing her the barrage of questions.

Inside, the station hummed with activity. Kent led her through a maze of corridors to a small, sparsely furnished room where evidence from the case was being catalogued and examined. On a central table lay items seized from Nora's lodgings: the violin case, sheet music, newspaper clippings, and most damning of all, the small glass vial containing traces of a clear liquid.

"May I?" Mildred gestured toward the evidence.

Kent hesitated, then nodded to the constable on duty. "You may examine the items but not handle them directly. Standard procedure."

Mildred bent over the table, studying each piece carefully. The violin case was well-worn but lovingly maintained, typical of a dedicated musician with limited means. The newspaper clippings were unremarkable, though their collection did suggest a fixation on Anton's death that might seem suspicious.

It was the vial that drew her closest attention. Small, brown glass, with a handwritten label bearing the words 'Potassium Cyanide Solution' in careful script. The constable obligingly turned it with gloved hands, allowing Mildred to view it from all angles.

"This label," she said suddenly. "It's not what I would expect."

Kent moved closer. "How so?"

"It's too neat, too legible. Most chemical labels in laboratories or pharmacies are printed, or if handwritten, done by someone accustomed to labelling dozens of vials daily. This has the careful precision of someone deliberately trying to create a clear label."

Kent frowned. "That's hardly exculpatory. Perhaps Nora wanted to ensure she used the correct poison."

"Perhaps," Mildred conceded. "But may I see the label under stronger light?"

The constable brought over a desk lamp, positioning it to illuminate the vial. Under its harsh glare, Mildred leaned in, her gaze fixed on the edges of the paper label.

"There," she said softly. "Do you see it? The glue at the corners is still tacky. This label was applied recently, within the last day or two."

Kent bent to examine it himself, his professional scepticism momentarily giving way to genuine curiosity. "It could simply be poor-quality adhesive."

"Possibly," Mildred acknowledged. "But combined with the unusually clear handwriting and convenient placement in Nora's violin case, it suggests something else entirely."

"Planted evidence," Kent concluded reluctantly. "That's your theory?"

"It fits the facts better than Nora suddenly deciding to become a poisoner," Mildred replied. "Think about it, Inspector. If she had indeed poisoned Anton and kept this vial as some sort of trophy, why label it so clearly? Why not dispose of such damning evidence?"

Kent straightened, his expression troubled. "Even if the vial was planted, that doesn't necessarily prove her innocence. She could have used the poison and discarded the original container, only for someone else to plant this one to ensure her conviction."

"A possibility," Mildred conceded. "But unlikely. Nora is frightened and naive, not calculating. And who would want to frame her specifically?"

Before Kent could respond, a young constable appeared at the door. "Sir, the suspect is ready for questioning."

Kent nodded, then turned to Mildred. "I suppose you'll want to observe the interview."

"If you would be so kind."

With a resigned sigh that suggested he knew he would regret this concession, Kent led her to a small anteroom adjacent to the interrogation chamber. Through a narrow window, Mildred could see Nora seated at a table, her slender frame diminished by fear. The young violinist's face was pale with shock, her eyes red-rimmed from crying.

"Remember," Kent cautioned, "observation only. No interruptions."

Mildred nodded her agreement, though her mind was already cataloguing questions that Kent would likely overlook. She watched as he entered the interrogation room, his manner shifting subtly into the authoritative presence she had witnessed in previous cases.

"Miss Bellamy," he began, "can you explain how a vial of potassium cyanide came to be hidden in your violin case?"

Nora's voice trembled. "I can't, Inspector. It isn't mine. I've never seen it before. Someone must have put it there to... to make me look guilty."

"A convenient explanation," Kent observed, echoing his earlier comment to Mildred. "Yet we have witnesses who confirm your resentment toward Anton Lanyi after he withdrew your solo opportunity."

"I was disappointed, yes. Heartbroken, even. But I would never harm him!" Tears spilled onto Nora's cheeks. "He was my mentor, my inspiration. I wanted to play like him, not... not silence him forever."

"Then how do you explain the newspaper clippings about his death? Your landlady reports you've been obsessively following the case."

"Of course I have!" Nora's voice rose with a flash of indignation. "Everyone is talking about it. The whole musical community is devastated. And I... I keep hoping they'll find whoever really did this."

Mildred watched Kent's face closely. Despite his earlier certainty, doubt was beginning to creep into his expression. Nora's distress appeared genuine, her explanations, while convenient, also entirely plausible.

"Miss Bellamy," Kent continued, his tone softening slightly, "if someone did plant this evidence, can you think of who might wish to frame you? Who benefits from your arrest?"

Nora shook her head helplessly. "I don't know. I'm not important enough for anyone to target specifically. Unless..."

"Unless?" Kent prompted.

"Unless they simply needed someone to blame," she whispered. "Someone without powerful friends or connections. Someone dispensable."

The observation, in its plaintive simplicity, struck Mildred as potentially profound. If Anton's death was connected to something larger, as her discoveries suggested, then a quick resolution with a convenient scapegoat would serve many interests. Nora, young and vulnerable, with a publicly acknowledged motive, made an ideal candidate.

Kent continued the questioning for another twenty minutes, but Nora's story remained consistent. She had no knowledge of the vial, no explanation for its presence in her case, and no recollection of anyone who might have had the opportunity to plant it.

When Kent finally emerged from the interrogation room, his earlier certainty had visibly dimmed. He joined Mildred in the anteroom, closing the door behind him.

"Your thoughts?" he asked, in the tone of someone who already anticipated the response.

"The evidence was planted," Mildred stated firmly. "And rather clumsily at that. The question is not whether Nora is guilty, but who wants her to appear so."

Kent sighed, running a hand through his hair. "Even if I concede the possibility of planted evidence, I can't simply release her without further investigation. The superintendent is already preparing a statement for the press."

"Then give me twenty-four hours," Mildred urged. "Before you proceed with formal charges. Time to follow the thread of this planted evidence to its source."

For a long moment, Kent studied her face, weighing professional caution against their history of reluctant cooperation. Finally, he nodded once, curtly. "Twenty-four hours. But I'll need something concrete, not just intuition or speculation."

"Thank you, Inspector." Mildred gathered her coat and gloves, her mind already racing ahead to her next steps. "I'll contact you the moment I have something tangible."

As she prepared to leave, Kent added, "I hope you're right about her, Lady Mildred. For both your sakes."

The implied warning was clear. If Nora was indeed guilty, Mildred's intervention could be seen as obstruction. Her reputation, already skating the edge of propriety with her investigative activities, might not survive such a misstep.

Outside Scotland Yard, Mildred paused to collect her thoughts. The planted vial pointed to deliberate framing, but by whom? Someone with access to Nora's lodgings, knowledge of her relationship with Anton, and most importantly, a reason to divert suspicion from themselves or protect someone else.

The piano-tuner's key in her desk drawer, the coded notations in Anton's music, the whispers of smuggled valuables, the hollow violin case, all suggested a deeper conspiracy than a simple murder of passion or revenge. If Anton had indeed been transporting precious items across borders, his death might be connected to those activities rather than his musical relationships.

And if that were true, then whoever killed him would benefit greatly from Nora's conviction. A neat resolution, a closed case, and no further questions about hollow violin cases or coded sheet music.

The challenge now was to find concrete evidence linking the planted vial to the true killer, all within the twenty-four-hour window Kent had granted her. Mildred hailed a cab, her determination hardening into resolve. She would not allow an innocent young woman to become a convenient scapegoat, regardless of the risk to herself.

The game was more complex than even she had imagined, with stakes higher than professional pride or intellectual challenge. Somewhere in London, a killer was likely celebrating Nora's arrest, believing themselves finally safe from discovery.

They would soon learn otherwise.

17

A watery sun struggled through clouds as Mildred's cab pulled up outside Sylvia Harcourt's Belgravia townhouse. The elegant façade, with its pristine white columns and gleaming brass fixtures, gave no hint of the financial troubles rumoured to plague its owner. Mildred paid the driver and ascended the front steps, her mind focused on the task ahead: twenty-four hours to clear Nora's name, and Sylvia Harcourt was her most promising lead.

Her knock was answered by a solemn-faced butler, whose initial frostiness melted slightly at the mention of Lady Mildred's name. Society connections still carried weight, even in households teetering on the edge of ruin.

"Mrs Harcourt is indisposed, my lady, but I shall inquire if she might receive you."

Mildred was shown to a small anteroom while the butler disappeared upstairs. The space was impeccably maintained, yet subtle signs of decline were visible to her observant eye: a painting missing from a faded square on the wallpaper, silver candlesticks replaced by brass, fresh flowers arranged sparsely to disguise their modest quantity.

After several minutes, the butler returned. "Mrs Harcourt will see you in the morning room, my lady. Please follow me."

The morning room, bathed in the thin autumn light, was clearly Sylvia's refuge from encroaching troubles. Unlike the rest of the house, it retained its full complement of treasures: delicate porcelain figures, silver-framed photographs, and a particularly fine Constable landscape painting that Mildred recognised as a family heirloom.

Sylvia herself sat near the window, a writing desk before her covered with correspondence. She wore an elegant day dress in midnight blue, her blonde hair swept into a knot that emphasised the sharpness of her cheekbones. At Mildred's entrance, she rose with the practised grace of a woman accustomed to playing hostess, though strain showed in the tightness around her mouth.

"Lady Mildred, what an unexpected pleasure. I trust you're well?"

"Quite well, thank you," Mildred replied, taking the offered seat opposite Sylvia. "Though I confess my visit has a purpose beyond social niceties."

"Doesn't everything these days?" Sylvia's smile was brittle. "Tea, perhaps? Though I'm afraid we're economising on the biscuits."

"No, thank you. I've just come from Scotland Yard, where Nora Bellamy is being held for Anton's murder."

Sylvia's hand fluttered to her throat, a gesture that might have appeared genuine if Mildred hadn't been watching so intently. "How dreadful. Though I suppose the police must have their reasons."

"They believe they do," Mildred agreed. "A vial of cyanide

found in her violin case provides rather compelling evidence."

"Poor child. Though ambition can drive people to desperate acts." Sylvia's gaze drifted to the Constable landscape, as if seeking comfort in its familiar pastoral scene.

"Indeed it can," Mildred said softly. "As can fear of financial ruin."

The silence that followed was weighted with unspoken accusations. Sylvia's fingers drummed lightly on the arm of her chair, her composure cracking ever so slightly.

"I'm not sure I understand your meaning, Lady Mildred."

Mildred paused. She recalled the witness statements from backstage—the way several musicians had mentioned seeing Mrs Harcourt lingering near the costume racks after most had dispersed, her nervous habit of wringing her gloves, the slight hesitation when the subject of Anton's withdrawal from her patronage was raised at Lady Ivy's breakfast. Then there were the words spoken by Bea only that morning: "Sylvia was burning papers in her bedroom, Millie, and Lady Westmorland's maid swears she was sobbing before the concert began."

Mildred's mind lined up the cues: the freshness of the vial's label and glue, so recently affixed it left a faint tackiness on her glove; Nora's unmistakable distress, genuine confusion, and open panic during her own questioning; Mrs Harcourt's access to Nora's instrument case as a patroness with backstage privilege—not to mention her known desperation over vanished fortunes.

"I think you do, Mrs Harcourt. The vial in Nora's case had a newly applied label. The glue was still tacky. Someone planted that evidence quite recently, someone desperate to direct suspicion away from themselves."

Sylvia's laugh was unconvincing. "And you imagine I had something to do with this? Really, Lady Mildred, I may not be as wealthy as I once was, but I hardly go about planting poison vials in young ladies' violin cases."

"Perhaps not under ordinary circumstances," Mildred conceded. "But these are hardly ordinary times for you, are they? Your investments have failed, your creditors are circling, and Anton Lanyi was threatening to break his contract with you, which would have been the final blow to your already precarious finances."

Sylvia's face paled. She rose abruptly and walked to the window, her back to Mildred as she gathered herself. When she turned, the society mask had slipped, revealing naked fear beneath.

"How could you possibly know all that?"

"London's drawing rooms are full of whispers, Mrs Harcourt. And I have a particular talent for listening."

For a long moment, Sylvia seemed to waver between continued denial and confession. Finally, her shoulders sagged in defeat. She returned to her chair, sitting heavily, the graceful patroness suddenly diminished to a frightened woman.

"It's worse than they say, you know," she began, her voice low. "My husband left me comfortably provided for, but not extravagantly so. I made investments, hoping to maintain our lifestyle. South American rubber, African mining ventures, Russian bonds before the revolution. Each failed more spectacularly than the last."

"And Anton's patronage was a significant expense," Mildred prompted gently.

"Yes, but a necessary one. In society, one's association with brilliant artists is currency. His concerts gave me entrée to circles that would otherwise have closed against me. I could not afford to lose him." Her fingers twisted nervously in her lap. "But Anton was becoming... difficult. Demanding renegotiation of terms, threatening to accept Lady Ivy's patronage instead."

"He knew about your financial troubles?"

Sylvia nodded miserably. "He discovered some papers in my desk when I stepped away during a meeting. After that, he began to hint that he might expose my situation unless I agreed to more favourable terms. My reputation would have been ruined. The last of my credit would have evaporated overnight."

"A powerful motive," Mildred observed. "Did you poison him, Mrs Harcourt?"

"No!" Sylvia's denial was vehement. "I considered it, God help me. I even acquired the means. But I couldn't go through with it. I'm a coward, Lady Mildred, not a murderer."

"But you did plant the vial in Nora's case," Mildred stated, not as a question but a certainty.

The fight seemed to drain out of Sylvia. She nodded almost imperceptibly. "After Anton's death, I was terrified. The police were asking questions, examining everyone's movements. I still had the poison I'd obtained, and I knew it would incriminate me if discovered."

"So you created a convenient scapegoat."

"I needed someone with a plausible motive," Sylvia admitted, shame colouring her words. "Everyone knew Anton had promised Nora a solo, then withdrawn it. And she's so young, so... expendable. No powerful family to protect her, no social connections to shield her."

"Unlike yourself," Mildred noted, unable to keep disapproval from her tone.

"Yes," Sylvia whispered. "I know how despicable it sounds. But I was desperate. When I learned the police were planning to search the musicians' lodgings, I saw my chance. I still had a key to the rehearsal rooms from my patronage duties. It was simple enough to slip the vial into her case while she was practising."

"And the newspaper clippings? Were those your additions as well?"

Sylvia nodded. "A final touch of obsession. I thought it would make her appear fixated on Anton's death."

Mildred studied the woman before her, feeling a complex mixture of pity and disgust. Sylvia Harcourt was not evil, merely weak. Faced with the collapse of everything she valued, she had chosen self-preservation over justice.

"You do realise that your actions have placed an innocent young woman at risk of hanging," Mildred said, her voice gentle but firm.

Tears welled in Sylvia's eyes. "I didn't think it would go so far. I thought the police would merely question her, perhaps hold her briefly. By the time it became serious, I expected them to find the real killer." She brushed the tears away with an impatient hand. "What will you do now? Tell Inspector Kent?"

"I must," Mildred replied. "Nora's freedom depends on it."

"Then I am ruined," Sylvia said with quiet resignation. "My reputation, my standing, all gone. Perhaps prison awaits."

"Planting false evidence is a serious matter," Mildred agreed, "but not as serious as murder. If you cooperate fully, tell Inspector Kent exactly what you've told me, your punishment may be mitigated."

"And if I refuse?" A flash of defiance crossed Sylvia's face.

"Then I shall present my observations about the freshly glued label, along with the testimony of your butler, who will undoubtedly confirm your absence from the house during the time the evidence was planted." Mildred's tone remained conversational, but her resolve was clear. "One way or another, Mrs Harcourt, the truth will emerge. The question is whether you wish to salvage some small measure of dignity by confessing voluntarily."

Sylvia was silent for a long moment, considering her options. Finally, she nodded. "Very well. I shall accompany you to Scotland Yard and make my statement. Allow me time to change into something appropriate for public disgrace."

As Sylvia left to prepare herself, Mildred remained in the morning room, contemplating the Constable landscape painting. It would likely be sold soon, along with the remaining treasures, to satisfy creditors. A family legacy scattered to the winds, much like Sylvia's reputation.

Yet for all the pathos of Sylvia's situation, Mildred could not forget Nora sitting in a cell at Scotland Yard, her dreams and career in jeopardy due to Sylvia's cowardice. The planting of evidence revealed desperation, but not the will to kill. If Sylvia had not killed Anton, then who had? And why?

The puzzle remained incomplete. Sylvia had provided one crucial piece, clearing Nora of suspicion, but the central mystery still loomed. Who had applied the poison to Anton's tonic bottle with such precision that it activated only when uncorked? Who had both the knowledge of his habits and the opportunity to tamper with his preparation?

Sylvia returned wearing a sombre grey ensemble, her face composed behind a delicate veil. "I'm ready, Lady Mildred."

Together they departed the Belgravia townhouse, its elegant façade now seeming like a theatrical backdrop for the real drama unfolding behind its doors. In the cab to Scotland Yard, Sylvia sat in silence, occasionally dabbing at her eyes with a lace handkerchief.

"There is one more thing I should ask you," Mildred said as they neared their destination. "In your capacity as Anton's patroness, did you ever observe anything unusual about his violin case? Or perhaps hear him mention smuggling valuable items across borders?"

Sylvia's hand stilled, the handkerchief suspended midway to her face. "How did you know about that?"

"Then it's true?"

A bitter smile curved Sylvia's lips. "Why do you think I was so desperate to maintain our arrangement? Anton's concerts were profitable in ways beyond mere ticket sales and social standing. He transported certain items for me. Small, valuable pieces that could be discreetly sold abroad or brought back to England, bypassing customs and taxes."

"Smuggling," Mildred clarified.

"A harsh word for a necessary arrangement," Sylvia countered. "But yes. Anton's hidden compartment carried more than sheet music on our Continental tours."

"And did others know of this arrangement? Otto Klein, perhaps? Or Maestro Moretti?"

Sylvia hesitated, clearly weighing how much more to reveal. "Otto knew, certainly. He was Anton's constant companion. As for others... I couldn't say for certain. Anton was not as discreet as one might hope. He enjoyed having secrets, and sometimes hinted at them to feel important."

The cab pulled up outside Scotland Yard, ending their conversation. As they prepared to disembark, Sylvia clutched Mildred's arm suddenly.

"Lady Mildred, there's something else you should know. I was not Anton's only... client in these matters. There were others, people with more to lose than I, people who might resort to more permanent solutions if their arrangements were threatened."

"Do you know who these people might be?" Mildred asked urgently.

"No names. Anton was careful about that. But he mentioned a title, someone with diplomatic connections. And he was frightened in his final weeks. He told me he wanted out, that things had gone 'too deep.' I thought he meant our contract, but perhaps..."

Her words trailed off as a constable approached to assist them from the cab. The moment for further revelations had passed, but Sylvia's final disclosure had opened new avenues of inquiry. If Anton had been involved in smuggling for multiple clients, including someone with diplomatic immunity, and had decided to extricate himself from these arrangements, it provided a far more compelling motive for murder than artistic jealousy or financial pressure.

As they entered Scotland Yard, Mildred reflected that Sylvia's half-confession had cleared one mystery only to deepen another. Nora would soon be free, but the true killer remained at large. And somewhere in London, someone with powerful connections might be watching Mildred's investigation with growing concern, realising that the convenient arrest of Nora Bellamy had failed to end the hunt for Anton Lanyi's murderer.

The game was not over. It had merely entered a more dangerous phase.

18

The morning after Sylvia's confession brought a pale sun that did little to warm the chilly October air. Mildred stood at her study window, watching a pair of sparrows quarrel over crumbs on the garden wall. Her thoughts, however, remained fixed on the case. Sylvia Harcourt would face consequences for planting evidence, but her actions had merely obscured the true killer's identity rather than revealed it.

Nora had been released from custody with an apology from Inspector Kent that Mildred suspected cost him considerable professional pride. The young violinist's relief had been palpable, though her ordeal had left shadows beneath her eyes. "What happens now?" she had asked, clutching her belongings in the police station foyer. Mildred had no ready answer. The case had grown more complex with each revelation, and the hunt for Anton's killer seemed to touch on matters far beyond a simple musical rivalry.

The telephone's shrill ring interrupted her reflections. Perkins appeared moments later, his normally impassive face betraying concern.

"Inspector Kent on the telephone, my lady. He says it's a matter of some urgency."

Mildred hurried to her desk, lifting the receiver with a sense of foreboding. Kent's voice came through crisply, dispensing with pleasantries.

"There's been an incident at Volkov's workshop. I thought you might want to see it before my men finish processing the scene."

"What sort of incident?" Mildred asked, already reaching for her coat.

"Vandalism, at first glance. But targeted, not random. I'll explain when you arrive."

Twenty minutes later, her cab pulled up outside the luthier's modest establishment in Camden. A police constable stood guard at the door, acknowledging Mildred with a nod as Kent emerged to greet her.

"Thank you for coming so promptly," he said, guiding her inside. "I wanted your perspective before we draw conclusions."

The sight that greeted them was one of methodical destruction. The workshop that had been crowded but orderly during Mildred's previous visit, now resembled the aftermath of a whirlwind. Tools lay scattered across the floor, workbenches had been overturned, and violin parts splintered beneath their feet. What struck Mildred most, however, was not the chaos but the precision behind it. This was no random act of vandalism. Every drawer had been emptied, every cabinet searched, every potential hiding place examined.

"Someone was looking for something specific," she observed, carefully picking her way through the debris.

"My assessment as well," Kent agreed, watching her navigate the space. "Though what that might be remains unclear. Volkov claims nothing valuable was taken, despite the extensive damage."

"Where is he now?"

"Being treated for minor injuries at the hospital. He interrupted the intruder and received a blow to the head for his trouble. He'll recover, but he was quite shaken."

Mildred knelt beside an overturned cabinet, her gaze catching something in the dust that had settled on the floor. A footprint, small and distinctly feminine, with a faint chip on the right heel.

"Inspector," she called softly, "would you look at this?"

Kent joined her, crouching to examine the impression. "A woman's shoe, narrow heel. And there's a chip or break in the heel edge."

"Exactly. Not what one would expect from a common burglar."

Kent's gaze met hers, the unspoken question hanging between them. Could Sylvia Harcourt have ransacked Volkov's workshop after her confession? It seemed unlikely. She had been in police custody, preparing her formal statement about the planted evidence. Besides, what could she hope to find here?

"Let's not jump to conclusions," Kent cautioned, as if reading her thoughts. "A broken heel is hardly definitive evidence. Half of London women probably have similar damage to their shoes."

"True," Mildred conceded, "though it does suggest our intruder was not who we might initially suspect."

They continued their examination of the workshop, noting further signs of the meticulous search. A wall of shelves held dozens of small drawers, each labelled with types of wood, tools, or components. Every drawer had been pulled out and upended, their contents scattered like autumn leaves.

"Something is odd about this damage," Mildred noted, crouching to examine a violin that had been split nearly in two. "It feels... performative. As if the vandalism is meant to disguise the true purpose of the search."

Kent nodded, impressed despite himself. "I had the same thought. Too thorough, too deliberate. Someone wanted us to believe this was simple destruction, but their real target was something specific."

"The hollow violin cases," Mildred suggested. "Volkov admitted he built the secret compartment in Anton's case. Perhaps there were others."

"Or documentation of what those compartments might have contained," Kent added. "Records, perhaps, of items smuggled across borders."

The alliance between them, however temporary, felt comfortable in its familiarity. For all their disagreements, they shared a mutual respect that surfaced in moments like these, when the puzzle took precedence over professional boundaries.

"I'd like to speak with Volkov when he's recovered," Mildred said. "He knows more than he's admitted. I'm certain of it."

"I've arranged for him to give a statement tomorrow morning," Kent replied. "You're welcome to attend, though in an unofficial capacity, of course."

"Of course," Mildred echoed with the ghost of a smile. Their dance of formality and collaboration had its own rhythm by now, steps both familiar and cautiously maintained.

As they prepared to leave, Mildred cast a final glance around the devastated workshop. Something about the scene nagged at her subconscious, a detail or connection just beyond her grasp. The footprint with its broken heel, the targeted search, the deliberate destruction, all pointed to something larger and more complex than mere vandalism or theft.

"One moment," she said, returning to the footprint. "May I borrow your pencil, Inspector?"

Kent handed it over with a raised eyebrow. Mildred carefully traced the outline of the shoe's impression on a piece of paper from her notebook, paying particular attention to the distinctive chip in the heel.

"For comparison," she explained, tucking the drawing away. "Should we encounter our mysterious lady elsewhere."

Outside, the autumn air was sharp with the promise of rain. Kent escorted Mildred to the main road, where cabs could be easily hailed.

"What's your next step?" he asked, his professional curiosity evident.

"I have an engagement at Lady Ivy's literary salon this afternoon," Mildred replied. "Perhaps society gossip will yield insights that physical evidence cannot."

Kent's expression suggested scepticism, but he had learned not to underestimate the value of Mildred's social connections. "Keep me informed, will you? Officially, this case remains unsolved, despite Miss Bellamy's release and Mrs Harcourt's confession."

"Of course, Inspector," Mildred assured him. "We both want the same outcome, after all."

Though privately, she wondered if that were entirely true. Kent sought closure within the bounds of law and procedure; Mildred pursued truth wherever it led, even into uncomfortable territories that challenged social hierarchies and official narratives.

———

Lady Ivy Carrington's literary salon proved to be exactly as Mildred had anticipated: a gathering of London's intellectually fashionable, more interested in being seen appreciating literature than in the literature itself. The drawing room of Ivy's Mayfair mansion buzzed with conversation, champagne flowed freely despite the early hour, and a nervous young poet stood neglected in the corner, his latest work largely ignored.

Mildred circulated with practised ease, exchanging pleasantries while her gaze swept the room for useful information. Lady Ivy herself held court by the fireplace, resplendent in jade silk and gleaming pearls.

"Mildred, darling!" she exclaimed, extending bejewelled fingers. "I was beginning to think you'd abandoned us for your detective work. Everyone's talking about your role in clearing that poor violinist girl. Such drama!"

"Hardly dramatic," Mildred demurred, accepting a glass of champagne from a passing footman. "Simply a matter of observing the evidence carefully."

"Well, I hear Inspector Kent is positively furious that you upstaged Scotland Yard yet again," Ivy said with evident delight. She leaned closer, her voice dropping to a conspiratorial whisper. "Is it true you found poison in Sylvia Harcourt's possession? I always said she had a touch of the femme fatale about her."

Mildred smiled noncommittally. "I'm afraid the details must remain confidential while the investigation continues."

"Of course, of course," Ivy waved a dismissive hand. "Though you must admit, it's all terribly thrilling. First Anton dropping dead mid-concert, then poor Nora arrested, now Sylvia implicated. One wonders who might be next!"

The gleam in Ivy's eye suggested she rather hoped it would be someone in her own social circle, providing fresh material for her salon conversations. Mildred was about to excuse herself when a slender woman in a modest grey dress approached, carrying a leather portfolio.

"I beg your pardon, Lady Ivy, but the invitations for next week's musicale require your approval."

"Ah, Miss Winters," Ivy declared. "My dear friend Sir Basil has been most generous in lending me his secretary to help organise today's event. Where would I be without her? Do excuse me, Mildred. Duty calls, tedious though it may be."

As Ivy turned her attention to the papers Miss Winters presented, Mildred found her gaze drawn to the secretary's shoes. They were practical black leather, polished to a modest shine, with narrow heels typical of a working woman's practical elegance. What caught Mildred's interest, however, was a small repair to the right heel, a nearly invisible patch where a chip had been mended with professional care.

Mildred reached for her notebook, comparing the drawing she had made of the footprint in Volkov's workshop. The size and shape seemed similar, though Miss Winters' right heel showed a careful repair; the workshop print had been made by a heel still chipped, not yet mended.

Miss Winters glanced up, catching Mildred's scrutiny. A faint flush coloured her cheeks, but her composure remained intact. "Is something amiss, Lady Mildred?"

"Not at all," Mildred replied smoothly. "I was admiring your shoes. So practical yet elegant. Might I ask where they were repaired? The craftsmanship is excellent."

The question, innocent on its surface, landed with unexpected weight. Miss Winters' hands tightened on her portfolio, her knuckles whitening briefly before she regained control.

"Barton's on Marylebone High Street," she answered, her voice steady. "They're quite reasonable for minor repairs." Mildred filed it away as confirmatory of the repair—and therefore no proof of the workshop print.

"Indeed? I must remember that. One does go through so many heels in London." Mildred smiled pleasantly, though her mind was racing with implications. Miss Winters' mended heel made the likeness tempting, but inconclusive; if anything, it suggested the workshop intruder had worn a heel not yet repaired. The better question was why someone wanted that impression noticed.

The remainder of the salon passed in a blur of conversation and observation. Mildred noted that Miss Winters remained close to Lady Ivy throughout, efficient and unobtrusive, yet somehow more present in Mildred's awareness than she had been before. Once or twice, their eyes met across the room, a fleeting acknowledgement that something had shifted between them.

As the gathering began to disperse, Mildred found herself beside Miss Winters in the entrance hall, collecting their coats.

"You seem remarkably interested in footwear today, Lady Mildred," Miss Winters observed quietly. "One might almost suspect it goes beyond fashion concerns."

The directness surprised Mildred. She studied the secretary's face, finding intelligence and wariness in equal measure. "One notices details in my line of work," she replied. "Especially when they connect to other observations."

A shadow passed across Miss Winters' features, quickly controlled. "I imagine you see connections everywhere. Though not all are what they first appear."

Before Mildred could respond, Lady Ivy's voice rang out from the drawing room, calling for her secretary. Miss Winters offered a polite nod and turned away, her posture betraying no hint of the tension Mildred had glimpsed moments before.

Outside, the afternoon had darkened, clouds gathering for an imminent downpour. Mildred opened her umbrella just as the first heavy drops began to fall, her thoughts as turbulent as the weather. The repaired heel created a tantalising connection, but to what end? Was Miss Winters involved in Anton's death, or merely in the subsequent attempts to obscure evidence? And what was her relationship to Lady Ivy, whose own interest in the case seemed to extend beyond mere social gossip?

The footprint in Volkov's workshop, the meticulous search, the repaired heel, all added new dimensions to an already complex puzzle. Yet Mildred couldn't shake the feeling that she was being led down a carefully constructed path, seeing connections that had been deliberately placed for her to find.

As her cab navigated the rain-slicked streets toward home, Mildred resolved to learn more about Miss Winters. If the secretary had indeed ransacked Volkov's workshop, she was either directly involved in Anton's death or working on behalf of someone who was. Either way, the repaired heel offered a thread that, carefully followed, might lead to the heart of the mystery.

But a nagging doubt persisted. The connection seemed almost too convenient, too easily discovered. Was Miss Winters truly careless enough to wear the same shoes to Lady Ivy's salon? The repaired heel and the still--chipped print felt too neat to be fate; if Miss Winters figured at all, it was as a distraction. The footprint's story, not its owner, would lead further in.

The answer, Mildred suspected, lay not in what had been taken from Volkov's workshop, but in what the intruder had hoped to find. And that, she was increasingly certain, connected to the hollow violin case and whatever secrets it had once contained.

19

The rain that had persisted through the night finally abated by mid-morning, leaving behind a glistening London and a crisp autumnal clarity. Mildred was enjoying a late breakfast when the telephone rang with unusual urgency. Perkins answered it, his face taking on that particular expression he reserved for calls from Scotland Yard.

"Inspector Kent for you, my lady," he announced, somehow conveying both disapproval and resignation in a single sentence. "He seems rather... agitated."

This was unusual. Kent prided himself on maintaining composure, particularly in professional matters. Mildred took the receiver, immediately alert.

"Inspector? Good morning."

Kent's voice crackled through the line, pitched lower than usual but vibrating with barely contained fury. "It's gone. The violin. Anton Lanyi's Guarneri has vanished from the evidence room."

Mildred's hand tightened on the receiver. "When?"

"Sometime overnight. The constable on duty swears it was there at midnight when he logged the evening inventory. By morning shift change, it had disappeared."

"It was being held onsite at the Royal Albert Hall," Kent added, anticipating her question. "The insurance underwriters demanded further documentation before it could be officially moved to Scotland Yard—their examiner was due this morning to make a final assessment for the claim, and Volkov was set to verify the instrument's condition for the museum trustees. The superintendent thought it safer to leave it in the Hall's secure office under double guard, rather than risk transporting it through the night until the formalities were complete. Only a handful of people had access."

Mildred could hear the frustration in his tone. "Red tape and a quarter-million-pound violin—now vanished, and not a note out of place where the case should have been."

"Was anything else taken?"

"No. Not the case, not the sheet music, not a single other piece of evidence. Just the violin itself." The frustration in Kent's voice was palpable. "I need your assistance, Lady Mildred. Immediately."

She raised an eyebrow, though he couldn't see it. "My assistance? This is a rather dramatic change of heart, Inspector."

"This isn't the time for pleasantries or point-scoring," Kent replied sharply. "A quarter-million-pound instrument has disappeared from police custody. The Commissioner is breathing fire, and I have a roomful of suspects but precious little time to interrogate them all properly."

"I'll come at once," Mildred promised, curiosity overtaking any desire to prolong Kent's discomfort. "Scotland Yard?"

"Royal Albert Hall," Kent corrected. "We're retracing every possible path the violin could have taken. I've summoned all relevant personnel from the night of the concert."

Twenty minutes later, Mildred's cab pulled up outside the concert hall, where two police automobiles were already parked. The grand building looked strangely diminished in the harsh morning light, its evening glamour replaced by the mundane reality of delivery vans and maintenance workers.

Inside, Kent had commandeered the administrative offices. A makeshift investigation room had been established, with constables coming and going, telephones ringing, and a palpable atmosphere of barely controlled chaos. In the centre of it all stood Kent, his normally immaculate appearance showing signs of a sleepless night—his tie slightly askew, his hair ruffled from running his hands through it.

"Lady Mildred," he acknowledged, gesturing her into a side office where they could speak privately. "Thank you for coming so promptly."

"Of course," she replied, studying his face. "Though I confess I'm curious about the sudden desire for my involvement."

Kent's expression tightened momentarily, then relaxed into resigned pragmatism. "You have insights into this case I cannot afford to ignore. And unlike my superiors, you understand the significance of the violin beyond its monetary value."

"You believe it's connected to the smuggling operations?"

"I'm certain of it. Why steal a violin that can never be publicly sold? Its provenance is too well-documented, its distinctive features too recognisable. No reputable dealer would touch it."

Mildred nodded thoughtfully. "Unless what matters isn't the instrument itself but something hidden within it."

"Precisely. Something small enough to conceal inside a violin. Perhaps what was originally transported in the case's hidden compartment." Kent leaned against the desk, fatigue momentarily visible in the slump of his shoulders. "We've been focusing on the case all this time, but what if the violin itself contained another hiding place?"

The possibility sent a ripple of excitement through Mildred. "Have you questioned Volkov about this?"

"He claims to know nothing about modifications to the violin, only the case. Though given the state of his workshop after the break-in, I'm inclined to believe him."

"And the theft itself? Do you have any suspects?"

Kent's expression darkened. "One. Arthur Pike, the stage manager. He had access to the building, knowledge of the security protocols, and a set of master keys that could open nearly any door in the hall."

"Including the evidence room?"

"Not officially, but a determined man with Pike's experience could manage it. We've brought him in for questioning, but he's denying everything." Kent straightened, professional resolve reasserting itself. "Would you like to observe the interview? Your knack for noticing... inconsistencies might prove valuable."

The concession clearly cost Kent some pride, but Mildred appreciated the gesture. "I'd be glad to help."

They made their way to what had once been the conductor's private room, now repurposed as an interrogation space. Through a partially open door, Mildred could see Arthur Pike seated at a small table, a cup of untouched tea before him. He was a sturdy man in his fifties, with the weathered hands of someone who had spent decades moving scenery and managing the physical elements of theatrical productions.

Most notably, attached to his belt was an enormous ring of brass keys—dozens of them, large and small, all jangling slightly whenever he shifted position. The very picture of a man with access to every locked door. Yet the overnight evidence ledger shows no authorised opening of the secure cabinet, narrowing the window and pointing to an alternative route—the north service corridor and linen chute.

"He's been carrying that keyring for twenty years," Kent murmured as they observed from the doorway. "Claims he can identify each key by touch alone, even in the dark. Useful skill for a stage manager during performances."

"And rather damning in the current circumstances," Mildred observed.

"Indeed. Shall we?"

Kent entered first, with Mildred following discreetly to sit in a corner of the room. Pike glanced up, his expression hardening when he recognised Kent but shifting to curiosity when he noticed Mildred.

"Mr Pike," Kent began, "I believe you understand why you've been asked to come in today."

"Something about a missing fiddle," Pike replied, his voice gruff but steady. "Though why you think I'd know anything about it is beyond me."

"You were here last night."

"I'm here most nights. That's my job."

"And you possess keys that could access the secure room where the violin was being held."

Pike's hand moved instinctively to his keyring. "I've got keys to storage rooms, utility closets, dressing rooms. Nothing that would open police locks."

"Are you certain about that?" Kent pressed. "In twenty years, you've never acquired a key that might open a secure cabinet?"

"Look, Inspector," Pike leaned forward, his weathered face creased with exasperation. "I unlock doors for musicians who've forgotten their passes. I help stagehands access equipment. I don't break into evidence rooms and steal priceless instruments."

As the interview continued, Mildred studied Pike carefully. His indignation seemed genuine, his bewilderment at being a suspect, unfeigned. And yet, something about the situation nagged at her. If Pike hadn't taken the violin, who had? And how had they accessed the secure room?

Her gaze wandered around the conductor's room, taking in details that others might overlook. The ornate moulding around the ceiling. The antique furniture, slightly worn at the arms. The small service door near the corner, presumably connecting to corridors used by staff to move discreetly through the building during performances.

"Mr Pike," she interrupted suddenly, "could you tell me about the service passages in the hall? Where do they lead?"

Both men turned to look at her, surprised by the question.

"Service passages?" Pike repeated, brow furrowing. "Well, they connect most of the main areas. Dressing rooms to the stage, administrative offices to the public areas. Helps staff move about without disturbing the audience."

"And do these passages connect to the room where the violin was being kept?"

Pike considered this, fingers absently tracing patterns on the tabletop. "Not directly, no. But the north corridor runs behind that section of the building. There's a laundry chute nearby for sending soiled linens down to the basement."

"A laundry chute," Mildred echoed, an idea forming. "Large enough for a violin?"

"Probably, though it would be a tight fit. And risky for an instrument like that."

Kent was watching her intently now, sensing the direction of her thoughts. "You're suggesting someone used the service passages to access the area, then sent the violin down the chute to an accomplice?"

"It would explain how the violin disappeared without any doors being unlocked," Mildred replied. "And why Mr Pike's keys, impressive though they are, may not be relevant to this particular mystery."

Pike's relief was visible, though he tried to maintain a gruff exterior. "I told you I had nothing to do with it. Why would I risk my position here? Twenty years I've worked in this hall."

"Then perhaps you'd be willing to show us these service passages," Kent suggested, his tone marginally less accusatory. "Particularly the location of this laundry chute."

"Gladly, if it clears my name."

They followed Pike through a labyrinth of narrow corridors hidden behind the public spaces of the Royal Albert Hall. These utilitarian passages, with their plain walls and practical lighting, provided a stark contrast to the opulence of the concert spaces. Pike moved through them with the confidence of long familiarity, occasionally pointing out features of interest.

"Main electrical controls there... costume storage through that door... and here's the linen service area."

They emerged into a small room lined with shelves of folded towels and tablecloths. In one corner stood a large metal door set into the wall, hinged at the bottom to create a chute.

"This goes down to the laundry room in the basement," Pike explained. "Used mostly for napkins and table settings after receptions, sometimes performers' robes if they need cleaning."

Mildred approached the chute, examining it carefully. It was indeed large enough to accommodate a violin, though as Pike had noted, sending such a valuable instrument down would be risky. As she knelt to look more closely at the metal doorway, something caught her eye: a few tiny threads of crimson velvet clinging to the edge of the opening.

"Inspector," she called softly, "would you look at this?"

Kent joined her, crouching to examine what she had found. "Fibres," he confirmed. "Red velvet."

"The same material used to line Anton's violin case," Mildred noted. "Though the violin itself was not in its case when it disappeared, was it?"

"No. The violin and case were being examined separately." Kent straightened, his expression thoughtful. "Someone wrapped the violin in similar material to protect it before sending it down the chute."

"Which suggests planning and care, not opportunistic theft," Mildred concluded.

Pike, watching this exchange with growing concern, shifted uncomfortably. "I swear I had nothing to do with this. I don't even have access to that fancy velvet stuff."

"No," Kent agreed, studying the man with a more measured gaze. "But someone in this building does. Someone who knew about the service passages, the laundry chute, and the precise location of the violin."

Mildred's mind was already racing ahead. "We should examine the basement immediately. And check whether anyone unusual was seen entering or leaving the building last night."

As they made their way downstairs, Mildred noticed Kent watching her with an expression that mingled frustration and reluctant admiration.

"You've done it again," he remarked quietly, as Pike led the way through another service corridor.

"Done what, Inspector?"

"Seen what the rest of us overlooked. Those fibres could have been there for weeks, and yet you connected them immediately to the missing violin."

Mildred smiled slightly. "Perhaps because I wasn't distracted by an obvious suspect with a conspicuous ring of keys."

Kent conceded the point with a wry nod. "Sometimes the most visible solution is deliberately placed to draw attention away from the truth."

"Like a magician's flourish with one hand while the other performs the actual trick," Mildred agreed. "Though in this case, I suspect our real thief is far more subtle than a stage illusionist."

The basement laundry room was cavernous and humid, filled with industrial washing equipment and the clean, sharp scent of soap. Several workers looked up in surprise as the unusual trio entered—a police inspector, a society lady, and the stage manager, all clearly on a mission.

"Has anyone seen anything unusual come down the laundry chute in the past twelve hours?" Kent asked without preamble. "Something that shouldn't have been there?"

The workers exchanged glances, until one elderly man stepped forward. "There was a bundle came down around one this morning. Wrapped in red cloth, it was. Thought it odd, since we don't use red linens for anything."

"And what happened to this bundle?" Mildred asked gently.

"Young woman came for it not five minutes later. Said it was a mistake, costume department meant to send it to repairs, not laundry. Took it away before anyone could say much about it."

Kent's posture stiffened. "A young woman? Can you describe her?"

The laundry worker shrugged. "Ordinary sort. Dark hair, neat clothes. Had a slight limp, though. Remember thinking she'd have trouble with the stairs, carrying whatever it was."

Mildred and Kent exchanged a significant look. "It could be Miss Winters or any number of women with a temporary limp," Kent said at last. "The repaired heel you noticed means her shoe was already mended; our intruder's heel might not have been."

"Treat the limp as suggestive, not probative,' Mildred murmured. "Let the route and fibres do the talking."

"Thank you," Kent told the worker. "You've been most helpful."

As they left the laundry room, Pike trailing behind them like a confused but relieved shadow, Kent spoke in a low voice to Mildred. "Miss Winters, Lady Ivy's secretary. The repaired heel you noticed."

"It seems a remarkable coincidence," Mildred agreed. "Though we should be careful not to leap to conclusions. The heel may yet be another red herring, deliberately placed to mislead us."

"Perhaps," Kent conceded. "But it gives us a direction to pursue." He turned to Pike, who had been listening with mounting confusion. "Mr Pike, you're free to go. Though I'd appreciate your discretion regarding this matter."

"Of course, Inspector. My lips are sealed." Pike hesitated, then added, "For what it's worth, I hope you find that violin. Beautiful instrument. Made music like I've never heard before or since."

As the stage manager departed, jangling his massive keyring as if to remind them of his innocence, Kent turned to Mildred. "What now? Miss Winters seems the obvious next step, but if she's merely a pawn in a larger game..."

"Then we need to understand who's moving the pieces," Mildred finished. "The violin's disappearance confirms that something valuable is hidden within it—something worth the risk of stealing from police custody."

"But what? And for whom?"

These questions hung between them, unanswered for now. The missing violin had added another layer to an already complex puzzle. Someone had gone to elaborate lengths to retrieve it, using the building's own infrastructure to avoid detection. The same someone, perhaps, who had arranged Anton Lanyi's death when he threatened to end their arrangements.

As they emerged into the concert hall's grand foyer, sunlight streaming through the high windows, Mildred found herself wondering about the violin's journey. From Anton's hands to the police evidence room, then wrapped in velvet and sent down a laundry chute to be collected by a woman with a distinctive limp. Where was it now? And what secret did it contain that was worth a virtuoso's life?

The game had escalated, moving from murder to theft, from suspicion to certainty. Somewhere in London, Anton's violin was being carefully examined—not for its priceless craftsmanship, but for whatever treasure lay hidden within its wooden heart.

20

Rain pattered steadily against the windows of Mildred's study as she reviewed her notes on the missing violin. The discovery of velvet fibres at the laundry chute had established a new direction for the investigation, but questions still outnumbered answers. If Miss Winters, with her distinctive limp and repaired heel, had indeed collected the instrument, she was likely acting on someone else's behalf, but whose?

A light tap at the door announced Perkins, who entered bearing a silver tray with a letter.

"This just arrived by special messenger, my lady. The delivery person was most insistent it reach you without delay."

Mildred accepted the cream-coloured envelope, noting the distinctive letterhead of Lloyd's of London, the insurance underwriters. Inside was a brief note requesting her presence that afternoon regarding "a matter of mutual interest concerning the late Mr Anton Lanyi's violin."

"How intriguing," she murmured. "Perkins, please telephone

Lady Beatrice and ask if she might join me for a visit to Lloyd's this afternoon."

"Very good, my lady."

After Perkins departed, Mildred sat back, turning this new development over in her mind. Insurance companies rarely involved themselves in police matters unless significant sums were at stake. The Guarneri violin was certainly valuable, worth approximately a quarter of a million pounds by Kent's estimation, but why contact her rather than the inspector directly?

By two o'clock, Mildred and Bea were being shown into the imposing offices of Lloyd's of London. The building exuded quiet wealth and stability, with its polished mahogany panels and portraits of stern-faced founders gazing down upon visitors.

"Rather intimidating, isn't it?" Bea whispered, adjusting her hat nervously. "Like being summoned to the headmistress's office, only with more money at stake."

Mildred smiled at the comparison. "Let's hope we're not about to be scolded for misbehaviour."

Their escort, a junior clerk in an impeccably pressed suit, led them through corridors lined with discreet doors until they reached a conference room where two men awaited. The older gentleman rose at their entrance, bowing slightly.

"Lady Mildred Ramsay, Lady Beatrice Mortimer. Thank you for coming on such short notice. I am Gerald Hargreaves, senior adjuster, and this is my colleague, Mr Phillips."

Phillips, a thin man with wire-rimmed spectacles and ink-stained fingers, nodded without rising from his seat, where he appeared engrossed in a substantial file of papers.

"Thank you for your invitation, Mr Hargreaves," Mildred replied, taking the offered chair. "Though I confess I'm curious about why Lloyd's would contact me regarding Mr Lanyi's violin."

"Quite understandable." Hargreaves settled himself opposite them, folding his hands neatly on the table. "We understand you've been assisting Inspector Kent in his investigation, albeit unofficially. Your reputation for discretion and insight has reached us through certain channels."

"How flattering," Bea remarked, though Mildred detected a note of wariness beneath her friend's light-hearted tone.

Hargreaves smiled thinly. "Indeed. We find ourselves in something of a delicate situation. The violin in question was insured through Lloyd's for a substantial sum. The policy was taken out not by Mr Lanyi himself, but by his patroness, Mrs Sylvia Harcourt."

"I see," Mildred said, filing away this information. "And now that the violin has disappeared from police custody, the claim has been activated?"

"Precisely." Phillips looked up from his papers for the first time, his voice unexpectedly resonant for such a slight man. "Mrs Harcourt filed the claim yesterday morning, stating that as the instrument was now missing, she was entitled to the full insured value."

"That seems straightforward enough," Mildred observed. "Why involve me?"

Hargreaves exchanged a glance with Phillips before continuing. "We have certain... concerns about the circumstances. Mrs Harcourt took out this policy only three months ago, significantly increasing the coverage from its previous level. Moreover, while the violin was comprehensively insured against loss, theft, or damage, Mr Lanyi himself was not."

"No life insurance?" Bea asked, surprised.

"None through our firm, and we've checked with other major insurers as well. Given Mrs Harcourt's financial patronage of Mr Lanyi, one might have expected both the musician and his instrument to be protected."

Mildred considered this carefully. "You suspect fraud?"

"We suspect irregularities, Lady Mildred," Hargreaves corrected diplomatically. "Mrs Harcourt's financial difficulties are not unknown to us. Several of her properties were recently mortgaged to their full value, and her investments have performed poorly. The insurance payout for the violin would represent a substantial windfall at a very convenient time."

"Especially if she had a hand in ensuring its disappearance," Mildred concluded.

Phillips nodded vigorously. "Exactly so. We cannot make such accusations officially without evidence, but before processing a claim of this magnitude, we must investigate thoroughly."

"And what would you like from me?" Mildred asked, though she had already guessed the answer.

"Your insights, Lady Mildred. Your observations about Mrs Harcourt, her relationship with Mr Lanyi, and any connection she might have to the violin's disappearance. We understand from Inspector Kent that you witnessed certain events firsthand."

For the next hour, Mildred recounted her observations of Sylvia Harcourt, from the concert through to her confession about planting evidence on Nora Bellamy. She described

Sylvia's whispered conversation with her solicitor, her visible anxiety throughout the evening, and her admission regarding Anton's smuggling activities.

"So Mrs Harcourt was aware that Mr Lanyi used his violin case to transport valuables?" Phillips interrupted, scribbling furiously in a notebook.

"Yes, though she claimed it was primarily the case, not the violin itself, that contained the hidden compartment. Volkov, the luthier, confirmed this."

"And yet it's the violin that has now vanished, not the case," Hargreaves mused. "Curious."

"The case remains in police custody," Mildred confirmed. "Though its hidden compartment was empty when discovered."

As the interview continued, Mildred found herself increasingly convinced that Sylvia's motives were indeed financial, though not necessarily murderous. The patroness had been desperate enough to plant evidence on an innocent young woman, but that spoke of opportunism rather than premeditated malice. And while she might have arranged for the violin's theft to claim the insurance, that didn't explain Anton's poisoning.

"There's something else you should know," Mildred added as the meeting drew to a close. "The night before last, Volkov's workshop was ransacked. Someone was searching for records of the modifications he made to instrument cases, including Anton's."

Hargreaves raised an eyebrow. "That suggests a connection to the smuggling operation rather than merely an insurance fraud."

"Precisely my thought," Mildred agreed. "If Sylvia is involved in the violin's disappearance, I suspect it's as part of a larger scheme, not simply for the insurance payout."

As they prepared to leave, Bea, who had been uncharacteristically quiet throughout the meeting, suddenly spoke up. "Mr Hargreaves, do you insure other musical instruments as well? Pianos, perhaps? Or even tea shops?"

The question seemed so incongruous that even Phillips looked up from his papers in surprise.

"Well, yes, Lady Beatrice. Lloyd's insures a wide variety of properties and valuables. Though I'm not sure I understand the connection to tea shops."

"Oh, I was just wondering," Bea continued airily, "whether one might insure a bun shop against, say, excessive consumption by greedy customers. My aunt Agatha runs one in Bath, you see, and she's forever complaining about gentlemen who eat more than they pay for."

There was a moment of startled silence before Phillips let out a sudden bark of laughter, quickly stifled behind his hand. Hargreaves' mouth twitched despite his obvious attempt at professional composure.

"I fear such losses would fall under expected operating expenses rather than insurable risks, Lady Beatrice. Though your aunt's predicament does sound most vexing."

Bea sighed dramatically. "I shall tell her to install smaller chairs, then. Make it uncomfortable to linger too long over the Chelsea buns."

This practical solution proved too much for the junior clerk, who had been waiting by the door. He dissolved into poorly concealed laughter, earning a reproving glance from Hargreaves that did little to dampen the moment of levity.

As they departed Lloyd's imposing offices, Mildred gave her friend an appreciative look. "Bun shops and greedy gentlemen? Really, Bea?"

"They were all so dreadfully serious," Bea defended herself. "And that poor clerk looked ready to expire from boredom. Besides, it's always useful to see how people react to unexpected humour. Did you notice how Phillips actually smiled? I'd wager he's more amenable to unorthodox theories than his superior."

"Your methods of character assessment continue to surprise me," Mildred acknowledged with a smile. "Though I'm not sure how they advance our understanding of Anton's murder or the missing violin."

"Perhaps not directly," Bea conceded as they hailed a cab, "but at least we know Sylvia had a tangible financial motive for wanting the violin to disappear. A quarter of a million pounds would solve her money troubles quite handily."

Inside the cab, sheltered from the persistent drizzle, Mildred turned this new information over in her mind. "The timing is certainly suspicious. Increasing the insurance coverage just three months before Anton's death, ensuring the violin was protected but not the musician himself."

"She could have arranged the theft," Bea suggested. "Though that doesn't explain the murder. Unless..."

"Unless she feared Anton would expose the scheme?" Mildred finished the thought. "Possible, though it seems an extreme response to insurance fraud. The penalties for that are severe, but not as severe as those for murder."

"Perhaps the two events aren't directly connected," Bea proposed. "What if Sylvia saw an opportunity in Anton's death? She didn't kill him, but once he was gone, she arranged for the violin to disappear, knowing she could claim the insurance."

"Opportunistic rather than premeditated," Mildred nodded. "That aligns with her character as we've observed it. Desperate enough to seize advantages, but perhaps not cold-blooded enough to plan a murder."

The cab rattled through London's wet streets, its windows streaming with rain that transformed the passing scenery into impressionistic blurs of light and colour. Mildred's thoughts, however, remained crystal clear, focused on the web of motives and opportunities surrounding Anton's death and the violin's disappearance.

"If Sylvia arranged the theft," she reasoned aloud, "she would need an accomplice with access to the police evidence room. Someone who knew about the service passages and the laundry chute."

"Miss Winters?" Bea suggested. "The secretary with the repaired heel?"

"Possibly, though I'm not convinced she's working for Sylvia. Their social circles don't seem to overlap significantly."

"Then who is she working for?"

This question lingered between them as the cab approached Mildred's home. The missing violin, the insurance policy, the ransacked workshop, the mysterious secretary, all formed pieces of an increasingly complex puzzle. Sylvia's financial motive provided one clear thread, but Mildred sensed it was just one strand in a more intricate tapestry of deception.

That evening, as Mildred sat by the fire reviewing her notes, she received a telephone call from Inspector Kent.

"We've located Miss Winters, Sir Basil's secretary," he informed her without preamble. "She was seen boarding a train to Dover this morning. By the time my men arrived, she had already sailed for Calais. It is not yet confirmed she was aboard."

"Fleeing the country," Mildred mused. "That certainly suggests guilt, though not necessarily on whose behalf."

"There's more," Kent continued, his voice tight with controlled frustration. "We've received information that a violin matching the description of Lanyi's Guarneri was transported across the Channel today, carried by a diplomatic courier with immunity from searches."

"A diplomatic courier?" Mildred sat up straighter. "That connects to what Sylvia mentioned about Anton's clients including someone with diplomatic connections."

"Precisely. And it places the violin well beyond our reach, at least for now."

The implications were clear. Someone with considerable influence had orchestrated the violin's theft and subsequent removal from British jurisdiction. But was this the same person who had arranged Anton's murder? And where did Sylvia Harcourt fit into this increasingly international intrigue?

"What about Sylvia's insurance claim?" Mildred asked.

"Suspended pending investigation, according to Lloyd's. She's reportedly quite distraught, claiming she had nothing to do with the theft."

"And you believe her?"

Kent paused, considering. "I'm not certain. Her financial motive is clear, but the diplomatic connection suggests something larger at work. Something that might have begun as insurance fraud but connects to Anton's smuggling activities and, ultimately, his murder."

As they ended their conversation, Mildred found herself returning to the image of the violin, now somewhere in France, carried by a diplomatic courier immune to ordinary laws. What was so valuable about that instrument that it warranted murder, theft, and international intrigue? The hollow case had been empty when discovered, but perhaps the violin itself contained another secret, one worth killing for.

Sylvia Harcourt's insurance scheme now seemed almost petty in comparison to the broader conspiracy taking shape. A desperate woman seeking financial salvation, she had become entangled in something far more dangerous than mere fraud. Whether victim or willing participant remained unclear, but one thing was certain: the mystery of Anton Lanyi's death and his vanishing violin had expanded beyond London's concert halls into the shadowy world of international diplomacy and secrets.

And somewhere within that web, the true killer waited, watching as suspicion fell on others, perhaps believing themselves beyond the reach of justice. Mildred, however, was not so easily deterred. The violin might have vanished across the Channel, but the trail of evidence remained, and she was determined to follow it to its conclusion, no matter how high or how far it led.

21

The discovery that Anton's violin had crossed the Channel under diplomatic protection left Mildred with a troubling sense that the case was growing beyond her reach. As much as she prided herself on understanding the complexities of London society, international diplomacy presented an altogether different challenge. Still, the core questions remained stubbornly unchanged: who had killed Anton Lanyi, and why?

She had arranged to meet Bea for lunch at Fortnum's, hoping her friend's irrepressible spirit might lift the fog of uncertainty that had settled over her thoughts. Bea arrived in a flurry of pale blue silk and animated chatter, perfectly timed to coincide with the arrival of their tea.

"You look positively funereal, darling," she announced, sliding into her chair with practised grace. "Has Inspector Kent been scolding you again?"

Mildred smiled despite herself. "Not scolding, precisely. But the violin's disappearance has complicated matters considerably. It seems to have been smuggled to France under diplomatic protection."

"How thrilling!" Bea exclaimed, helping herself to a cucumber sandwich. "International intrigue! Perhaps we should book passage to Paris. I've been longing for an excuse to visit the new Chanel boutique."

"I hardly think chasing smugglers across the Continent qualifies as a shopping expedition," Mildred replied dryly.

"Nonsense. Every adventure benefits from proper attire." Bea leaned closer, lowering her voice conspiratorially. "Besides, I have news that might interest you more than French fashion."

Mildred raised an eyebrow. "Oh?"

"I attended Lady Westmorland's musical soirée last evening. Nothing so grand as the Royal Albert Hall, of course, just a chamber ensemble. But guess who was performing?"

"I couldn't possibly."

"The second oboist from Anton's orchestra," Bea announced triumphantly. "A rather handsome fellow named Mr Bishop. We had a most illuminating conversation during the intermission."

"By 'illuminating,' I assume you mean you flirted shamelessly while extracting information," Mildred observed.

Bea looked momentarily affronted. "I merely expressed a sincere interest in the challenges of the oboe as an instrument. It's hardly my fault if he found my curiosity captivating." She adjusted her hat with an air of self-satisfaction. "In any case, he was quite forthcoming about the night of Anton's death."

"In what way?"

"Well," Bea said, selecting a dainty éclair, "it seems our friend Mr Klein was alone with Anton's violin case for several minutes before the performance. Mr Bishop mentioned it specifically because it struck him as unusual."

Mildred's attention sharpened. "Unusual how?"

"Apparently, while Anton was greeting admirers in the corridor, Otto took the violin case to the green room—alone and just before the second--half call. According to Mr Bishop, this broke their usual routine. Normally, Anton never let that case out of his sight."

"How long was Otto alone with it?"

"Long enough to be noteworthy, according to our oboist. Perhaps five minutes? When Anton returned, he seemed slightly agitated, though he calmed once Otto handed him his tonic."

Mildred sat back, absorbing this information. Otto Klein, alone with Anton's case shortly before the performance. Otto, who regularly prepared Anton's tonic. Otto, whose initials "O.K." appeared throughout Anton's coded annotations.

"Did your Mr Bishop mention anything else about that evening? Any unusual interactions between Anton and the other musicians?"

Bea's brow furrowed in concentration. "Let me think. He mentioned that Moretti was in a particularly foul mood, shouting at everyone about tempo and dynamics. And Sylvia Harcourt arrived looking 'positively green' around the edges. Oh, and apparently Nora was practising obsessively in a corner, though Anton barely acknowledged her."

"And Otto?"

"Calm as glass, according to Mr Bishop. 'Like a clockwork man,' were his exact words. Never showed a flicker of emotion, even when Anton collapsed."

This final detail settled in Mildred's mind like a key turning in a lock. Throughout their investigation, Otto Klein had been a quiet presence at the periphery, overshadowed by more dramatic suspects like the volatile Moretti or the financially desperate Sylvia. Yet he had been the closest to Anton, the most familiar with his routines, the one who prepared his tonic before every performance.

And now, it seemed, he had broken routine to be alone with Anton's case minutes before the fatal concert.

"Did your oboist friend mention seeing Otto with anyone else that evening? Perhaps having a private conversation with Moretti or Sylvia?"

Bea shook her head. "Not that he mentioned. Though he did say something curious about Otto's hands."

"His hands?"

"Yes. Apparently, oboe players notice such things. Mr Bishop said Otto's fingertips seemed stained, as if he'd been handling chemicals. He assumed it was some sort of pianist's remedy for calluses."

Chemical stains. Access to Anton's tonic. Time alone with the violin case. The pieces were beginning to align with disturbing clarity.

"You're thinking something frightfully serious, aren't you?" Bea observed, studying Mildred's face. "I can always tell by that little furrow between your eyebrows."

Mildred smiled faintly. "Just considering possibilities. Your Mr Bishop has provided some valuable insights."

"He's not 'my' Mr Bishop," Bea protested, though her cheeks flushed slightly. "Though he did invite me to another performance next week. Purely for musical appreciation, of course."

"Of course."

As they finished their luncheon, Mildred's mind continued to circle back to Otto Klein. Unlike the other suspects, whose motives were readily apparent – Moretti's artistic jealousy, Sylvia's financial desperation, Nora's thwarted ambition – Otto's motivations remained more obscure. Yet his opportunity was unmatched. As Anton's accompanist, he had the most intimate access to the violinist's routines and possessions.

What if Otto had used those five minutes alone with Anton's case to apply poison to the cork of his tonic bottle? A substance designed to activate only when the cork was removed? It would explain the precise timing of Anton's collapse, moments after taking his customary dose before stepping on stage.

But why? What could drive the seemingly loyal Otto to murder his longtime musical partner?

The answer, Mildred suspected, lay in those coded annotations with their recurring "O.K." notations. If they indeed referred to Otto Klein, perhaps they documented transactions or arrangements that had soured, threatening both men's security or reputation.

"You're miles away," Bea observed, interrupting her thoughts. "Should I be offended that my gossip has rendered me conversationally irrelevant?"

"Not at all," Mildred assured her. "Quite the opposite. Your information has given me much to consider."

"Enough to share with Inspector Kent?"

Mildred hesitated. While her suspicions about Otto were growing stronger, she remained wary of premature accusations. Kent would demand concrete evidence, not just circumstantial connections and second-hand reports from an oboist via Bea's flirtatious conversation.

"Not yet," she decided. "I need more than opportunity and possibility before approaching Kent. He's already sceptical of my theories about the violin case's significance."

"Well, while you're pondering," Bea said, signalling for the bill, "I have another tidbit that might interest you. Apparently, Moretti and Otto had quite a heated exchange after rehearsal the day before the concert. Mr Bishop couldn't hear the details, but he described it as 'unnervingly intense' coming from the usually reserved Otto."

This new detail added another wrinkle to Mildred's emerging theory. Could Moretti have been aware of whatever arrangements Otto and Anton were involved in? Perhaps even a participant himself? The conductor's gambling debts would certainly provide motivation for seeking additional income through less conventional means.

"Did he mention what happened after this exchange? Did they reconcile or remain at odds?"

"Oddly enough, they left together," Bea recalled. "Mr Bishop thought it peculiar, given the apparent animosity moments before. They walked out speaking in hushed tones, like conspirators rather than adversaries."

Conspirators. The word echoed in Mildred's mind as they departed Fortnum's and stepped into the autumn sunshine. Perhaps Otto and Moretti were both involved in whatever smuggling operation Anton had been conducting. If Anton had threatened to end these arrangements, as Sylvia had suggested, might both men have had reason to silence him?

Yet something about this theory felt incomplete. Moretti's temperament was too volatile for the methodical poisoning that had killed Anton. His rage expressed itself in public outbursts and theatrical gestures, not the careful application of poison to a tonic bottle's cork. If he were involved, it seemed more likely as an accessory or beneficiary rather than the killer himself.

Otto, on the other hand, possessed both the temperament and opportunity for such a calculating murder. His quiet demeanour, his precise habits, his intimate knowledge of Anton's routines, all painted the picture of someone capable of planning and executing such a crime.

As Mildred and Bea parted ways, Bea to a dressmaker's appointment, Mildred ostensibly homeward but with thoughts of a detour to the Royal College of Music to inquire about Otto's recent whereabouts, she found herself increasingly convinced of Otto's centrality to the case. Not only his potential guilt, but his connection to the missing violin and whatever secrets it contained.

Yet caution restrained her from sharing these thoughts, even with Bea. Too often in previous investigations, she had seen how premature accusations could alert the guilty or harm the innocent. Until she had more substantial evidence linking Otto to the poison that killed Anton, she would keep her suspicions private.

The busy London street offered anonymous passage as Mildred considered her next steps. If Otto Klein had indeed poisoned Anton Lanyi to protect some shared secret or arrangement, then he represented only one part of a larger conspiracy. The diplomatic courier who had transported the violin to France, Miss Winters with her repaired heel and mysterious connections, the ransacking of Volkov's workshop, all suggested an operation extending beyond the confines of London's musical community.

And somewhere within this web of intrigue, Maestro Moretti's role remained ambiguous. Was he simply a jealous rival, his artistic rage providing a convenient distraction from the real conspiracy? Or was he more deeply implicated, perhaps even working with Otto to eliminate Anton when he threatened their mutual interests?

The case had begun with a violin case's hollow sound and a virtuoso's sudden collapse. It now spanned international borders and diplomatic intrigue, with a missing violin that seemed to hold secrets worth killing for. Yet at its heart remained the fundamental questions of any murder: who had both motive and opportunity? Who stood to gain the most from Anton Lanyi's death?

The possibilities multiplied with each new piece of information, like variations on a musical theme. But Mildred was determined to follow the evidence to its conclusion, no matter how complex the composition proved to be.

22

Mildred sat at her desk, surrounded by the accumulating evidence of the case: notes in her careful handwriting, newspaper clippings about Anton's death, and most significantly, the sheets of music with their cryptic annotations that Otto Klein had given her at Claridge's.

That gesture now struck her as peculiar. If Otto truly had something to hide, why would he voluntarily provide her with what might be incriminating evidence? Perhaps the annotations contained nothing damning. Or perhaps they held secrets so cleverly concealed that he felt confident even her keen eyes would miss them.

Mildred adjusted her reading lamp and spread the pages before her. She had examined them multiple times since receiving them, initially focusing on deciphering the Hungarian phrases and the pattern of "O.K." notations. But now, with fresh insights from Bea's oboist friend about Otto's time alone with Anton's case, she approached them with renewed scrutiny.

"There's something here I've missed," she murmured to herself, reaching for her magnifying glass.

The annotations crowded the margins of the sheet music: Hungarian words, numeric sequences, and those recurring "O.K." markings that had initially drawn her attention. Some were written in blue ink, others in pencil of varying darkness. She had assumed the variations were due to Anton making notes at different times, perhaps over months or years of performing the same pieces.

But as she examined a particularly dense section of notes in the margin, something caught her eye. The quality of the pencil marks differed subtly. Most were soft-edged and slightly smudged, as one would expect from a musician making quick notes during rehearsal. But others—particularly several of the "O.K." notations—were sharper, darker, more deliberately formed.

"Different pencil," she whispered, leaning closer. "Different hand?"

She traced her finger along the sequence of annotations, noting which appeared original and which seemed added later. The pattern was subtle but unmistakable. The sharper notations appeared consistently near dates and locations: "Warsaw – 7/2," "Prague – 5/4," "Vienna – 14/3." Each accompanied by those telling "O.K." initials.

Mildred sat back, mind racing. What if the original annotations had been Anton's private code for his smuggling activities, with dates and locations but without explicitly naming his accomplices? What if someone had later added the 'O.K.' notations—almost certainly after the concert, given the torn fragment shows no such mark on the same margin?

The question was: who was being implicated, and by whom?

She reached for the torn scrap she had recovered from the concert hall on the night of Anton's death, carefully preserved in a separate folder. This fragment, unlike the pages Otto had given her, had been collected before anyone could have tampered with it. If her theory was correct, it should show the original annotations without the added markings.

With steady hands, she aligned the torn edge with its corresponding page in Otto's collection. The match was perfect, confirming they were indeed from the same original score. But where the page from Otto showed "Vienna – 14/3 – O.K." in dark, crisp pencil, the fragment showed only "Vienna – 14/3" in Anton's softer, more casual hand.

"Someone appears to have added these marks,' she concluded, a mixture of excitement and concern building within her. "But why? And what do they truly signify?"

The "O.K." could indeed refer to Otto Klein, creating a trail of evidence linking him to smuggling operations. But it could equally stand for "Old Key," "Outer Kontinent," or simply "Okay"—a confirmation that some transaction had been completed. Without the cipher key, the true meaning remained frustratingly elusive.

More troubling still was the possibility that someone was deliberately constructing a narrative. If the annotations had been altered, other evidence might have been tampered with as well. The entire case could be built on carefully crafted misdirection.

But who would have both the motive and opportunity to alter Anton's sheet music? Someone who knew about his smuggling operations. Someone who had access to his materials after his death. Someone who understood enough Hungarian to ensure the forgery wouldn't be immediately obvious.

The list of possibilities remained frustratingly broad.

Moretti? His explosive temperament made him an unlikely candidate for such meticulous deception, yet his artistic jealousy provided a compelling motive. And as conductor, he would have had access to Anton's sheet music.

Sylvia? Her desperate financial straits had already driven her to plant evidence on Nora. Might she also have tampered with these annotations to direct suspicion elsewhere? Her patronage certainly gave her access to Anton's materials.

Nora herself? The ambitious understudy, seeking to protect herself by implicating others? Yet her brief arrest suggested she was more victim than perpetrator.

Otto Klein? If the initials truly stood for something other than his name, he might have added them himself to create deliberate confusion. A masterful misdirection, hiding his guilt behind apparent evidence that seemed too obvious.

Miss Winters, with her repaired heel and diplomatic connections? If she had helped smuggle the violin to France, might she also have tampered with Anton's annotations to construct a narrative that served her employer's interests?

Arthur Pike, the stage manager with his massive keyring? Though cleared of stealing the violin, his access to the theatre's every corner made him an intriguing possibility.

Or Volkov, the luthier whose workshop had been ransacked? His technical knowledge would have made him intimately familiar with the smuggling operations, though the attack on his premises suggested he too was a target rather than an orchestrator.

A knock at the door interrupted her thoughts. Perkins entered, bearing a silver tray with the afternoon post and a telephone message.

"Inspector Kent telephoned, my lady. He asked if you might meet him at the Royal College of Music at four o'clock. He mentioned that they're continuing to gather evidence from Mr Klein's office."

"Thank you, Perkins. Please have the car brought around at half past three."

After the butler departed, Mildred returned to the annotated pages. Kent's focus on Otto's office suggested the inspector shared her interest in the accompanist, though perhaps for different reasons. But would he recognise the significance of these altered annotations, the possibility that someone was constructing a deliberate trail of evidence?

She carefully gathered the music sheets, the fragment, and her notes, securing them in a leather portfolio. Whether these alterations implicated or exonerated any particular suspect remained to be seen, but they undeniably revealed a calculated attempt to shape the narrative of Anton's activities and, by extension, his death.

The Royal College of Music stood serenely in the afternoon light, its Neo-Gothic façade revealing nothing of the investigation unfolding within. Mildred was directed to a small office on the second floor, where she found Kent supervising two constables as they methodically catalogued the contents of filing cabinets and drawers.

"Lady Mildred," Kent greeted her with a brief nod. "Thank you for coming so promptly. I thought you might find our discoveries of interest."

"You've found something significant?" she inquired, glancing around the modest space. Otto's office was neat and functional, with few personal touches beyond a framed photograph of a younger Otto and Anton outside a Viennese concert hall.

"Several things, actually." Kent gestured toward a small wooden box on the desk. "A rosin box. There's a crystalline residue inside; it's been sent to the laboratory. For now, treat it as provisional." He added, "The porter found the door standing ajar before we arrived, so we'll keep a scrupulous chain -of -custody from this point. No conclusions until the tests come back."

Mildred examined the box without touching it. "A damning find, certainly. Though perhaps too convenient."

Kent raised an eyebrow. "Too convenient?"

"It strikes me as careless for a murderer to keep poison in his office, especially one as meticulous as our killer appears to be. Unless, of course, he never expected his office to be searched."

"Or unless someone else placed it there," Kent concluded, following her reasoning with remarkable alacrity. "A rosin box with residue," Kent said. "We'll know what, precisely, when the lab reports."

Mildred glanced at the door. "Given the office wasn't sealed when the porter found it, anything discovered in plain view wants handling with tongs. Figuratively and literally."

Kent's mouth twitched. "Duly noted. Until we've dusted it and the tests are back, it's an open question whether it's evidence or someone's idea of it."

Mildred removed the annotated music and the hollow piano-tuner's key from her portfolio. "I've found something that complicates matters. This key, with its hidden compartment, parallels the violin case's design—both created for smuggling."

She explained her discovery, showing him the discrepancy between the fragment she had collected on the night of

Anton's death and the corresponding page in Otto's collection.

"You believe someone is deliberately creating a paper trail," Kent said slowly, studying the evidence.

"I believe someone is carefully constructing a narrative," Mildred corrected. "Whether to implicate Otto specifically or to obscure someone else's involvement, I cannot yet say. But the annotations were clearly altered after Anton's death."

Kent rubbed his chin thoughtfully. "The cyanide in this office seems straightforward enough. Yet I take your point about its convenience."

"Consider this, Inspector: if the killer truly is as calculating as the method of poison suggests, wouldn't they have disposed of incriminating evidence? Why leave poison where it could be found?"

"To frame someone else," Kent concluded. "Creating a trail so obvious that we couldn't help but follow it."

"Precisely. And if both the annotations and the poison were planted, we must ask ourselves: who benefits from directing suspicion toward Otto Klein?"

Their conversation was interrupted by one of the constables, who approached holding a small notebook. "Sir, I found this hidden behind the filing cabinet. Appears to be in code, but there are names and figures clearly visible."

Kent examined the notebook, then handed it to Mildred. The pages contained columns of numbers and initials, with occasional full names written in a cramped hand. Many entries were marked with a small circle—the same symbol that appeared in Anton's sheet music beside particularly significant annotations.

"A ledger," Mildred suggested. "Recording payments or shipments, perhaps."

"Some of these names are rather distinguished," Kent noted, pointing to several entries. "Members of Parliament, foreign diplomats. If they're involved in whatever smuggling operation Anton was running..."

"It could explain why the violin was removed under diplomatic protection," Mildred finished. "Someone powerful needed to ensure certain evidence never came to light."

As they continued examining the ledger, Mildred's mind returned to the altered annotations and their implications. If Otto was being framed, these discoveries in his office only strengthened the case against him. But if he was guilty, why would someone need to forge additional evidence? Unless, of course, the forgeries were meant to be discovered, casting doubt on legitimate evidence.

The complexity of the deception suggested a mind both calculating and desperate—qualities that could describe several of their suspects.

"What about Otto himself?" Kent asked suddenly. "Have you received any information about his whereabouts?"

"None," Mildred admitted. "Though his absence is telling in its own way."

"Indeed. A ferry ticket to Calais was found in his desk, dated the night the violin disappeared. Whether he fled to escape justice or was compelled to leave by other forces remains unclear."

This new piece of information shifted the kaleidoscope once more. Otto's apparent flight could indicate guilt, coercion, or an entirely different motivation. Without speaking to him directly, they could only speculate.

"What intrigues me most," Mildred said, "is not what we've found, but what we haven't. If Otto truly was involved in smuggling operations with Anton, where are the proceeds? His lifestyle is modest, his office simple. There's little evidence of wealth or extravagance."

"Perhaps he was merely a courier, not a beneficiary," Kent suggested. "Or perhaps his payment took a form we haven't yet identified."

"Or perhaps," Mildred added quietly, "he wasn't involved at all, and someone has gone to extraordinary lengths to make it appear as though he was."

As she gathered her portfolio to leave, having shared her findings about the altered annotations, Mildred felt a familiar mixture of excitement and frustration. The case was simultaneously clarifying and becoming more obscure, like a landscape alternately revealed and concealed by shifting fog.

The tampered annotations proved that someone was manipulating evidence, but whether to frame an innocent man or to strengthen the case against a guilty one remained unclear. The poison in Otto's office was either damning proof or a planted decoy. The missing violin held secrets that someone had gone to extraordinary lengths to protect.

And behind it all lurked the fundamental question: who had killed Anton Lanyi?

As she departed the college, stepping into the late afternoon sunshine, Mildred found herself recalling something her father had often said: "In a hall of mirrors, trust not what you see, but what you know to be true."

The evidence before her was a hall of mirrors, with truths distorted and reflections deliberately arranged to lead the eye astray. But somewhere within that labyrinth of deception lay a central truth, a solid fact that could not be altered or obscured.

Anton Lanyi had been poisoned by someone with intimate knowledge of his habits and access to his personal belongings. The violin had been stolen by someone who knew the building's hidden passages. The annotations had been altered by someone familiar with Anton's code and confident enough to believe the tampering would not be detected.

Whether these actions were performed by the same person or by a conspiracy of several remained to be seen. But Mildred was determined to unravel this web of manipulation, to distinguish genuine evidence from clever forgery, and to identify the true architect behind Anton's death—no matter how many false mirrors she had to shatter along the way.

23

The morning dawned with a pale sun that struggled through persistent cloud cover, casting Mildred's study in a gentle, diffused light. She sat at her desk, surrounded by the accumulating evidence of Anton's murder: the annotated sheet music with its mysterious tampering, newspaper clippings of the concert tragedy, and most significantly, a small glass bottle sealed in a handkerchief.

This bottle had occupied her thoughts since she had first noticed it near Anton's collapsed form. A simple tonic that, according to witnesses, he took faithfully before every performance. The same tonic that Otto Klein routinely prepared for him, which Anton uncorked himself precisely five minutes before stepping on stage.

The poison that killed Anton had been identified as potassium cyanide, but the precise method of its delivery remained elusive. Kent's investigation had focused on who might have tampered with the tonic itself, testing the remaining liquid for traces of poison. But something about this approach had never satisfied Mildred. If the liquid had been poisoned beforehand, why had Anton collapsed so suddenly, so precisely timed after taking his customary sip?

"There must be something we've overlooked," she murmured, turning the bottle carefully in her gloved hands.

A knock at the door announced Perkins with the morning post. "Dr Ainsworth telephoned, my lady. He can see you at eleven o'clock, as requested."

"Thank you, Perkins. Please have the car ready at half past ten."

After the butler departed, Mildred returned her attention to the tonic bottle. Kent had reluctantly allowed her to take it for 'unofficial consultation,' provided she maintained proper evidence protocols. Her friendship with Dr James Ainsworth, a distinguished chemist at University College London, might prove invaluable in understanding exactly how the poison had been administered.

At eleven precisely, Mildred was seated in Dr Ainsworth's cluttered laboratory. The elderly scientist peered at her over wire-rimmed spectacles, his bow tie slightly askew and his lab coat bearing the stains of countless experiments.

"Fascinating case, Lady Mildred," he remarked, carefully examining the tonic bottle. "Potassium cyanide is hardly a subtle choice of poison. Works rapidly, leaves distinctive traces. Not the weapon of someone hoping to evade detection."

"Yet the killer has evaded detection thus far," Mildred observed. "What particularly interests me is the timing. Anton took his tonic at exactly five minutes before performing, as was his routine. He stepped on stage, played brilliantly for several minutes, then collapsed suddenly. If the tonic itself was poisoned, why the delay in its effect?"

"An excellent question." Ainsworth held the bottle up to the light. "The police analysis found no trace of cyanide in the remaining liquid, I understand?"

"None. They concluded the poison must have been in the portion Anton consumed."

"Perhaps. But there are other possibilities." The chemist set the bottle down and reached for the cork, which had been preserved separately in a small glass container. "May I?"

Mildred nodded her assent, and Ainsworth carefully extracted the cork using tweezers. He examined it under a magnifying glass, turning it slowly to inspect every surface.

"Most interesting," he murmured. "The underside, where it contacts the liquid, appears slightly discoloured. Would you mind if I conducted a few tests?"

"That's precisely why I'm here, Dr Ainsworth."

For the next hour, Mildred watched as the chemist performed a series of meticulous analyses. He scraped minute samples from different areas of the cork, subjected them to various reagents, and observed the results with keen attention. His methodical approach reminded her of Kent's investigation techniques, though applied to chemical reactions rather than human motives.

Finally, Ainsworth looked up from his microscope, his expression animated with scientific excitement. "I believe I understand what happened, Lady Mildred. The poison wasn't in the tonic itself. It was applied to the underside of the cork."

"The cork?" Mildred leaned forward, intrigued.

"Precisely. A thin layer of potassium cyanide crystals was adhered to the bottom surface of the cork, the part that contacts the liquid when sealed. When Anton uncorked the bottle before his performance, the crystals dissolved into the top layer of the tonic. He then took his customary sip, ingesting the poison."

"But why didn't he taste it? Doesn't cyanide have a distinctive bitter almond odour?"

"It does to most people, though some cannot detect it, a curious quirk of nature. And the camphor in his tonic would have masked it quite effectively."

Mildred considered this revelation, her mind racing with implications. "So the poison was activated only when the cork was removed. Until that moment, the bottle had appeared perfectly innocent."

"Exactly. A clever method, requiring intimate knowledge of the victim's habits. Whoever did this knew Anton would uncork the bottle himself, take a sip, and then proceed to the stage. The delay between consumption and collapse was the time required for the cyanide to circulate—quickened by the exertion of performance, which hastened its fatal work."

"Which would depend on the dose and his physical activity," Mildred mused. "The exertion of playing the violin might have accelerated the poison's circulation."

"Quite so." Ainsworth carefully returned the cork to its container. "It's an elegant solution, in a macabre sense. The poison remains dormant until the very moment of use, leaving no opportunity for accidental discovery beforehand."

As Mildred departed the laboratory, her mind was filled with the implications of this discovery. The method of poisoning revealed something crucial about the killer: not just opportunity, but intimate knowledge of Anton's pre-performance ritual. Someone who knew he always uncorked the bottle himself, exactly five minutes before going on stage. Someone who understood that the bitter herbs in the tonic would mask the cyanide's taste.

In the cab returning to Mayfair, she reviewed the list of suspects through this new lens. Who had such precise knowledge of Anton's habits? Who would have had access to the cork before the performance?

Otto Klein seemed the most obvious candidate. As Anton's longtime accompanist, he was familiar with every aspect of the violinist's routine. He regularly prepared the tonic, though witnesses confirmed that Anton always uncorked it himself. But Otto wasn't the only possibility.

Moretti, as conductor, would have observed Anton's pre-performance habits over many concerts. He had been backstage that evening, though his whereabouts immediately before the performance were accounted for.

Sylvia Harcourt, as Anton's patroness, might have been privy to his rituals. She had admitted to planting evidence on Nora, showing a calculating side beneath her desperate exterior.

Nora herself had been backstage, nursing her disappointment about the withdrawn solo. But would she have had sufficient knowledge of Anton's precise timing?

And what about Arthur Pike, the stage manager with his massive ring of keys? His role required him to know everyone's movements and habits, though he seemed to lack a compelling motive.

Even Miss Winters, Lady Ivy's secretary with the repaired heel, remained a person of interest. Her connection to diplomatic circles and her apparent flight to France suggested involvement in the broader conspiracy, if not the murder itself.

The cab wound through London's busy streets, mirroring the circuitous path of Mildred's thoughts. The poisoned cork had eliminated some uncertainties while introducing new questions. It confirmed that the murder was premeditated, carefully planned by someone who understood not just opportunity, but chemistry and human habit.

Upon reaching home, Mildred found Bea waiting in the drawing room, her expression unusually serious. "There you are! I've been waiting positively ages. You'll never guess what I've heard about Otto Klein."

"What is it?" Mildred asked, setting down her handbag.

"He's been spotted in Paris. Mr Bishop, my oboist friend, has a cousin in the Paris Conservatoire who saw Otto at a café near the Sorbonne. He wasn't alone, Mildred. He was with a woman matching Miss Winters' description."

This new information sent a ripple of excitement through Mildred. Otto and Miss Winters together in Paris, presumably with Anton's stolen violin. But were they conspirators in murder, or merely participants in the smuggling operation that had surrounded Anton?

"There's something else," Bea continued, her voice dropping despite the empty room. "Mr Bishop mentioned Otto always carried a special rosin in a little wooden box—ritual rather than rarity, he said."

"A wooden box?" Mildred recalled Kent's discovery in Otto's office. "Like the one containing potassium cyanide?"

"I suppose it could be. Though Mr Hargreaves said there were several such boxes. One for rosin, one for spare strings, one for a special cloth Anton used to polish his violin. All part of the ritual."

Several boxes, all familiar components of a virtuoso's preparation. Any one of which could have been repurposed to hold poison. The picture was becoming clearer, yet simultaneously more complex. The method of murder pointed to someone intimately familiar with Anton's habits, but multiple suspects possessed that knowledge.

Mildred crossed to her desk and began writing a note to Inspector Kent, detailing Dr Ainsworth's findings about the poisoned cork. This crucial evidence would certainly advance the official investigation, though she suspected Kent might be reluctant to acknowledge the value of her 'unofficial consultation.'

As she wrote, Mildred found herself returning to the altered annotations in Anton's music. Those deliberate additions, made after his death, suggested someone was actively constructing a narrative about his activities and associates. Just as someone had carefully applied poison to a cork, knowing exactly how and when it would be used.

Both actions required precision, forethought, and intimate knowledge. Were they the work of the same hand?

"You've discovered something important, haven't you?" Bea asked, observing her friend's concentrated expression. "Something about how Anton died."

"The poison was on the cork," Mildred explained, setting down her pen. "Applied to the underside, so it would dissolve into the tonic only when Anton uncorked the bottle himself."

Bea's eyes widened. "How diabolically clever! That would explain why he didn't collapse immediately. But it also means..."

"It means the killer knew Anton's habits precisely," Mildred finished. "Knew he would uncork the bottle himself, exactly five minutes before going on stage. Knew the bitter herbs in the tonic would mask the cyanide's taste."

"That narrows our list of suspects considerably, doesn't it?"

"In some ways. But it also complicates matters. Several people had the necessary knowledge of Anton's routine. And someone has been actively manipulating evidence since his death, altering his annotations and possibly planting that cyanide container in Otto's office."

"Do you think Otto is guilty?" Bea asked directly.

Mildred hesitated, weighing the evidence. "He had the opportunity. The knowledge. Potentially the motive, if Anton was threatening to end their arrangements. But the deliberate tampering with evidence troubles me. Why alter annotations to implicate Otto if he was already guilty? It feels redundant."

"Unless someone wanted to ensure he took all the blame," Bea suggested. "Perhaps there were multiple people involved in whatever Anton was doing, and one decided to eliminate both Anton and Otto's credibility in a single stroke."

"That's quite perceptive, Bea," Mildred said, impressed by her friend's reasoning. "It would explain why Otto fled to Paris rather than staying to defend himself. He may be guilty of smuggling but innocent of murder, yet the evidence has been arranged to implicate him in both."

The two women sat in thoughtful silence, the ticking of the mantel clock the only sound in the elegant drawing room. Outside, London continued its bustling afternoon rhythm, oblivious to the web of deception and death they were untangling thread by thread.

Finally, Mildred sealed her note to Kent and rang for Perkins to have it delivered. "I believe we need to attend Lady Ivy's musicale tomorrow evening," she announced. "If Otto has been seen in Paris with Miss Winters, perhaps Lady Ivy knows more than she's revealed about her secretary's movements."

"A splendid idea," Bea agreed enthusiastically. "I shall wear my new blue gown. One should always look one's best when hunting for murderers in drawing rooms."

Mildred smiled at her friend's irrepressible spirit, but her mind remained fixed on the poisoned cork and what it revealed. The method was elegant in its precision, cruel in its calculation. It spoke of a mind that understood both chemistry and human habit, someone capable of turning Anton's own routine against him.

And as the afternoon light began to fade, casting long shadows across her study, Mildred wondered what other aspects of this case might reveal themselves under proper examination. Like the cork that appeared innocent until scrutinised by an expert, perhaps other seemingly mundane details held the key to identifying Anton's killer.

The musicale tomorrow might provide an opportunity to test certain theories, to observe reactions when Anton's tonic was mentioned. For despite the growing complexity of the case, one fact remained clear: whoever had applied poison to that cork had done so with deliberate intent and intimate knowledge of their victim's habits.

And such specific knowledge left a trail, if only one knew where to look.

24

Lady Ivy Carrington's musicale was the talk of London society that evening. Her Mayfair drawing room, transformed by candlelight and floral arrangements into an intimate concert venue, buzzed with anticipation and gossip in equal measure. The scandal of Anton Lanyi's death, Sylvia Harcourt's disgrace, and the missing violin provided irresistible conversational fodder for the city's elite.

Mildred arrived fashionably late, allowing her to survey the assembled guests before being noticed herself. Bea accompanied her, resplendent in the promised blue gown, which she wore with the casual confidence of a woman who knew precisely how well it suited her.

"Lady Mildred, Lady Beatrice!" Lady Ivy swept toward them, hands outstretched in greeting. "How divine of you to come. Everyone is absolutely agog about the latest developments in poor Anton's case. Is it true they found poison in Otto Klein's office? The whispers are positively electric!"

"I'm afraid I couldn't possibly comment on an ongoing investigation," Mildred replied with a pleasant smile.

"Though I'm certain Inspector Kent would be most displeased to hear of such leaks."

"Oh, discretion is so dreary," Lady Ivy pouted, then brightened. "But you simply must circulate. Maestro Moretti has honoured us with his presence, despite his grief. And little Nora Bellamy is here too, her first public appearance since that dreadful false arrest. Such courage!"

"How interesting," Mildred remarked, her attention sharpening. "I wasn't aware Nora had been invited."

"Last-minute addition to the programme," Lady Ivy explained with evident satisfaction. "The young pianist who was to accompany Signor Moretti developed a sudden malady—nerves, I suspect—and Nora stepped in. Talented girl, despite everything. And it adds such delicious drama to the evening, don't you think?"

Before Mildred could respond, Lady Ivy was swept away by other guests demanding her attention. Bea leaned closer, her voice low beneath the hum of conversation.

"Otto is supposedly in Paris, but Moretti and Nora are both here? How very convenient for your little experiment."

"Indeed," Mildred agreed. "Though I wonder about the timing of Nora's inclusion. Has she truly been rehabilitated so quickly after her arrest?"

"London society adores redemption stories almost as much as it relishes falls from grace," Bea observed. "And speaking of falls, there's Moretti by the champagne table, looking positively thunderous."

The Italian conductor stood apart from the crowd, a glass of champagne untouched in his hand. His expression was indeed stormy, his gaze fixed on Nora, who was conversing quietly with a group of musicians near the piano.

"Let's separate," Mildred suggested. "You engage Nora; I'll approach Moretti. We'll compare observations later."

Bea nodded, immediately adopting her most effervescent manner as she glided toward Nora and her companions. Mildred, meanwhile, made her way to the refreshment table, positioning herself within Moretti's orbit without directly approaching him.

As she selected a canapé, she casually removed a small glass bottle from her reticule and placed it on the table. It was nearly identical to Anton's tonic bottle, which remained in police evidence. She had obtained this replica from Dr Ainsworth, who had found it in his laboratory collection.

The bottle's placement was deliberate, visible but not conspicuous. Mildred moved away slightly, pretending to admire a nearby arrangement of orchids while keeping the bottle and Moretti in her peripheral vision.

The conductor's reaction was immediate, if subtle. His gaze darted to the bottle, then away, then back again with more focused attention. A slight tremor passed through his hand, causing a ripple in his champagne. He glanced around quickly, as if checking whether others had noticed the bottle's presence, then took a step closer to the table.

Mildred turned slightly, giving him a better view of her profile while still observing his movements. Moretti's face had paled beneath its natural olive tone, his lips compressed into a tight line. He seemed to be debating whether to approach the bottle or retreat from it.

Before he could decide, Lady Ivy's voice rang out, announcing the first performance would begin momentarily. Guests began migrating toward the arranged seating, creating a brief flow of movement around the refreshment table. When it cleared, Mildred noted with interest that the bottle remained in place, untouched.

Moretti, however, had positioned himself where he could keep it in view throughout the performance.

The first piece was a Debussy prelude, performed by Signor Moretti with evident technical skill if somewhat mechanical interpretation. Mildred found her attention divided between the music and the continued surveillance of her suspects.

Nora sat near the front, her posture rigid, hands clasped tightly in her lap. She would perform later in the programme, accompanying a soprano in several Schubert songs. From Mildred's vantage point, she could see that the young woman was far from the picture of rehabilitation Lady Ivy had painted. Her face was drawn, with shadows beneath her eyes suggesting sleepless nights.

As the prelude concluded and polite applause filled the room, Bea appeared at Mildred's side.

"Our little violinist is absolutely terrified," she whispered behind her fan. "Not of performing, mind you—she seems desperate to appear normal but keeps glancing toward the door as if expecting arrest at any moment."

"Interesting," Mildred murmured. "And did you mention the tonic bottle?"

"Most casually," Bea confirmed. "I remarked that Anton always took his special preparation before concerts, and wasn't it tragic how such a routine gesture became his last. She went quite pale and changed the subject immediately."

"Moretti had a similar reaction," Mildred noted. "Visible shock, though he's trying to mask it."

During the brief intermission between pieces, Mildred circulated among the guests, exchanging pleasantries while keeping the refreshment table in view. To her surprise, another figure approached the decoy bottle: Lady Ivy's secretary, Miss Winters.

"I thought she was in France," Bea whispered, materialising at Mildred's elbow.

"Apparently not," Mildred replied, watching as Miss Winters paused to straighten a scatter of glasses for the footman, her hand passing within inches of the bottle without touching it—efficient, unremarkable, and gone in a breath.

"Her heel is fully repaired," Bea observed. "No hint of a limp now."

Miss Winters departed the table without taking the bottle, but Mildred noted the slight tension in her shoulders as she walked away, suggesting awareness of being observed. The secretary disappeared into Lady Ivy's private study, presumably to attend to some hostess-related matter.

The second half of the programme featured Nora at the piano, accompanying a renowned soprano in Schubert's 'Gretchen am Spinnrade.' Despite her evident anxiety, Nora's playing was sensitive and technically assured, her fingers moving with the fluid precision of a true artist.

"She's really quite talented," Bea whispered. "Such a shame about the arrest business."

As the song concluded to enthusiastic applause, Mildred found her gaze drawn to Moretti once more. The conductor was not applauding. Instead, his attention remained fixed on the refreshment table—specifically, on the small glass bottle that continued to sit innocuously among the champagne flutes and canapés.

When the formal programme concluded, the guests dispersed into conversational groups while servants circulated with fresh champagne. Mildred made her way back to the refreshment table, noting with interest that the bottle remained untouched.

"Lady Mildred." Moretti's voice came from behind her, startling in its suddenness. "I was hoping to have a word."

She turned to find the conductor standing closer than expected, his dark eyes intense beneath heavy brows. "Maestro Moretti. I enjoyed your recent concert at Covent Garden. Your interpretation of Mahler was most affecting."

"You are too kind," he replied, though his tone suggested little interest in discussing Mahler. "I could not help but notice the bottle you placed on the table earlier. It resembles something that belonged to Anton."

"Does it?" Mildred kept her expression pleasantly neutral. "How observant of you."

"It is my business to observe details," Moretti said. "A conductor must see everything, hear everything. The police have Anton's tonic bottle in their evidence collection, do they not?"

"I believe so, yes."

"Then I am curious why you would bring a similar one to Lady Ivy's musicale." His voice lowered. "Unless it was to observe reactions. To see who might recognise it. A test, perhaps?"

Mildred met his gaze steadily. "An interesting theory, Maestro."

"Not a theory, Lady Mildred. A recognition of methodology. You have been investigating Anton's death, despite Inspector Kent's objections. You are looking for reactions, for signs of guilt. But remember, not all reactions indicate the same emotion. Recognition is not confession."

Before she could respond, Moretti gave a slight bow and moved away. The impression lingered—equal parts warning and challenge, the maestro staking his ground with theatrical candour.

As the evening progressed, Mildred observed both Nora and Miss Winters carefully. The young violinist seemed to be avoiding the refreshment table entirely, while the secretary moved through the room with professional efficiency, never allowing her gaze to linger on the bottle.

Bea, meanwhile, had taken it upon herself to become the evening's most exuberant guest, filling any conversational lulls with amusing anecdotes and drawing attention away from Mildred's quiet observations.

"And then," she was saying to a captivated group near the piano, "the ambassador's wife realised she'd been wearing her hat backward the entire evening! Can you imagine? Three hours at Buckingham Palace, and not a soul had the courage to tell her!"

The resulting laughter provided perfect cover for Mildred to retrieve her decoy bottle and return it to her reticule. As she did so, she felt rather than saw someone watching her—a prickling sensation at the back of her neck that she had learned never to ignore.

Turning slightly, she caught Miss Winters observing her from across the room. Their eyes met briefly before the secretary looked away, resuming her conversation with Lady Ivy as if nothing had happened.

The musicale concluded shortly before eleven, with guests departing in a flutter of silk wraps and murmured appreciation for the evening's entertainment. Mildred and Bea lingered deliberately, waiting until most had left before making their own farewells.

"Fascinating evening," Bea remarked as they waited for their car. "Three suspects, one decoy bottle, and enough tension to string a violin. Did you get what you wanted?"

"I believe so," Mildred replied thoughtfully. "The bottle provoked distinct reactions from Moretti, Nora, and Miss Winters. All recognised it, all were disturbed by its presence, but in subtly different ways."

"Moretti confronted you directly," Bea observed. "Rather bold for someone with something to hide."

"Or perhaps the boldest strategy of all," Mildred countered. "Acknowledging what others pretend not to see can be disarming. He's essentially saying, 'Yes, I recognise the bottle, but so what? That proves nothing.'"

"While Nora practically developed hives at the mere mention of Anton's tonic," Bea added. "Poor girl looked ready to faint when I brought it up."

"Fear, but is it guilt or trauma?" Mildred mused. "She was falsely arrested once; she may fear it happening again."

"And our mysterious Miss Winters? I thought Sir Basil's secretary was supposed to be in Paris with Otto."

"As did I," Mildred acknowledged. "Kent's report concerned a ticket, not a confirmed crossing; in any case, her presence here confirms she is back in London. Did she return alone, or is Otto also here?"

Their car arrived, and they settled into the back seat, Mildred quiet with contemplation, Bea still buzzing with the evening's social electricity.

"Well?" Bea prompted as they pulled away from Lady Ivy's residence. "Don't keep me in suspense. Who poisoned Anton's cork?"

Mildred gazed out at the darkened London streets, her mind piecing together the reactions she had witnessed with all the evidence gathered thus far: the poisoned cork, the tampered annotations, the hollow violin case, the smuggled valuables, the diplomatic connections.

"I believe I know," she said finally. "But I need one more piece of confirmation before I can be certain. The method of the murder is clear now—poison applied to the cork of Anton's tonic, designed to dissolve only when he uncorked it himself. That required intimate knowledge of his habits and access to his belongings."

"All three of our suspects had that," Bea pointed out.

"Yes, but only one of them reacted in a way that suggests not just recognition, but genuine shock at seeing what appeared to be the murder weapon in plain sight. Not guilt or fear of discovery, but something closer to disbelief. As if thinking, 'It cannot possibly be the same bottle, so why does it look identical?'"

"And that was...?" Bea leaned forward eagerly.

Mildred smiled slightly. "Patience, Bea. Let me confirm my suspicions first. But I believe we're very close to understanding exactly how Anton died, and more importantly, who arranged his final performance."

As their car continued through the lamp-lit streets of Mayfair, Mildred turned the decoy bottle over in her gloved hands, reflecting that sometimes the most revealing evidence was not what people did, but how they reacted when confronted with the unexpected. Tonight's experiment had confirmed her growing suspicion about which of their suspects possessed not just opportunity and motive, but the precise combination of knowledge, access, and calculation required to engineer Anton Lanyi's death with such deadly precision.

As Mildred set down her case notes, Perkins appeared with a telegram. "For you, my lady. It was delivered by hand."

She unfolded it, eyes narrowing as she read the spare message:

"Returning to London tomorrow. Will present myself for questioning to Inspector Kent. Truth must out. – O.K."

So Otto had decided to face the music after all. Whether compelled by guilt, loyalty, or something else remained to be seen—but at least he was prepared to meet his fate bravely or brazenly.

The puzzle was almost complete. One more piece, and the full picture would emerge—a composition of greed, betrayal, and murder orchestrated by a hand that had, until now, remained hidden in the shadows.

25

Lady Ivy's drawing room had never appeared more elegant than on this autumn afternoon. Sunlight streamed through tall windows, illuminating the cream and gold décor, glinting off silver tea services and crystal decanters. The setting seemed more suited to musical recitals or poetry readings than to the unmasking of a murderer, which was precisely why Mildred had selected it. Neutral ground, surrounded by the trappings of civilisation, would discourage unseemly outbursts when the truth was finally revealed.

"Everything is arranged exactly as you requested," Lady Ivy whispered, barely containing her excitement at hosting such a dramatic gathering. "The chairs are in a semicircle, the small table for your evidence. Though I still think we should have arranged for a photographer. Purely for posterity, you understand."

"Thank you, Lady Ivy," Mildred replied diplomatically. "But I believe Inspector Kent would object to turning a murder investigation into a society spectacle."

"So drearily official," Lady Ivy sighed, though her eyes sparkled with anticipation. "Still, I've told absolutely everyone that my drawing room was selected because of its perfect proportions for dramatic revelations. The acoustics are quite splendid, you know."

Mildred suppressed a smile as she arranged her portfolio on the small table at the centre of the room. Inside were the carefully preserved pieces of evidence she had gathered: the poisoned cork in its glass container, the annotated sheet music with its telling forgeries, the hollow piano-tuner's key, and Dr Ainsworth's detailed analysis of the poison's application method.

The guests began to arrive with punctual reluctance. Henry positioned himself near the door, a reassuring presence should difficulties arise. Bea swept in wearing a gown of rose pink that somehow managed to be both appropriate for a serious gathering and utterly frivolous. Inspector Kent arrived looking uncomfortable in his best suit, notebook already in hand, accompanied by a uniformed constable who remained discreetly in the hallway.

The suspects followed, each exhibiting their own form of nervous anticipation. Maestro Moretti entered scowling, his formal attire somehow more theatrical than practical. Sylvia Harcourt arrived with her solicitor, her former elegance diminished by recent scandal but still clinging to dignity. Nora Bellamy slipped in almost unnoticed, pale and drawn, taking a seat near the window as if contemplating escape. Miss Winters moved efficiently about the room, once again serving as Lady Ivy's assistant, though Mildred knew her true position was as Sir Basil's private secretary. Mildred noted her careful avoidance of the central table where the evidence lay.

True to his word and his telegram, Otto appeared in Lady Ivy's drawing room just as the clock struck, having returned from Paris with little more than a battered valise and the look of a man resigned to unpleasant necessity.

His willingness to face the assembled company, and perhaps the gallows, lent a gravity to the proceedings that even Mildred found unexpectedly affecting.

"Lady Mildred," he said softly. "An unexpected pleasure."

His composure was remarkable, considering he had only recently returned from Paris, where Bea's oboist friend had spotted him. Was it the confidence of innocence, or the calculation of a man who believed himself beyond suspicion? Mildred intended to discover which before the afternoon ended.

As everyone settled into their seats, an expectant hush fell over the room. Lady Ivy positioned herself slightly apart, ostensibly supervising the tea service but clearly unwilling to miss a moment of the drama. Miss Winters stood by the door, her posture rigid, her repaired heel no longer betraying any hint of its former damage.

Mildred moved to the centre of the semicircle, conscious of every eye upon her. Inspector Kent sat to her right, notebook open, his expression professionally neutral though his posture suggested heightened alertness.

"Thank you all for coming," she began. "I realise this is an unusual gathering, but the circumstances of Anton Lanyi's death have been equally unusual. What first appeared to be a tragic but straightforward poisoning has revealed itself as something far more complex—a carefully orchestrated murder connected to a web of smuggling operations and deliberate misdirection."

She removed the first piece of evidence from her portfolio: Dr Ainsworth's report on the poisoned cork. "Anton died from potassium cyanide poisoning, as we all know. What remained unclear until recently was exactly how the poison was administered. The police investigation found no trace of cyanide in the remaining tonic, suggesting Anton had consumed the poisoned portion."

Kent nodded in confirmation, his gaze sweeping across the assembled suspects, assessing their reactions.

"However," Mildred continued, "further examination of the cork itself revealed a different mechanism. The poison was applied to the underside of the cork, designed to dissolve into the tonic only when Anton uncorked the bottle himself, five minutes before going on stage, as was his invariable routine."

A murmur rippled through the room. Moretti leaned forward, brow furrowed. Nora twisted her handkerchief nervously. Otto remained still, only his eyes moving as they followed Mildred's presentation.

"This method required intimate knowledge of Anton's habits," Mildred explained. "Not just access to his belongings, but understanding of his precise timing, his consistent ritual of uncorking the bottle himself, and awareness that the bitter herbs in his tonic would mask the taste of cyanide."

She placed a second item on the table: the annotated sheet music. "Throughout this investigation, we've encountered evidence that has been deliberately altered. These musical annotations, for example, show clear signs of tampering. Original notes made by Anton have been supplemented with additional markings, particularly the initials 'O.K.' beside dates and locations that correspond to smuggling operations."

"Smuggling?" Lady Ivy couldn't contain herself. "How absolutely scandalous!"

"Indeed," Mildred agreed, turning slightly to include her in the conversation. "Anton Lanyi was using his position as a touring virtuoso to transport valuable items across borders, concealed in a specially modified compartment in his violin case. This operation involved several participants and beneficiaries, creating a complex network of shared secrets and mutual vulnerability."

She gestured toward the hollow piano-tuner's key. "Items like this, dropped by someone fleeing a music shop near the Thames, were ingeniously designed to conceal diamonds, documents, even microfilm. The piano-tuner's key is particularly clever; its legitimate purpose grants the carrier access to concert halls worldwide, while its hollow chamber smuggles valuables worth thousands. The smuggling operation itself is not our primary concern today, though it provides essential context for understanding the motive behind Anton's murder."

Inspector Kent shifted slightly in his chair. "We have confirmed through diplomatic channels that such operations were indeed occurring. Several prominent individuals have already been questioned in relation to these activities."

"The question before us," Mildred continued, "is who poisoned Anton's tonic cork, and why. The method tells us several important things about the killer: they had access to potassium cyanide, intimate knowledge of Anton's pre-performance routine, opportunity to handle the tonic bottle before the concert, and a compelling motive to silence Anton permanently."

She paused, allowing the weight of these requirements to settle upon the assembled suspects. Each would now be mentally assessing their own vulnerability, measuring themselves against the criteria she had established.

"Let us consider each suspect," Mildred said, her voice measured and calm. "Maestro Moretti certainly had grievances against Anton, both artistic and financial. Their rivalry was well-known in musical circles."

Moretti stiffened, his dark eyes flashing with indignation. "It was a professional disagreement, nothing more."

"Perhaps," Mildred conceded. "Yet your outburst after rehearsal, overheard by several musicians, suggested intense personal animosity. However, your whereabouts immediately before the performance are well-documented. You were conducting final preparations with the orchestra, making it nearly impossible for you to have accessed Anton's tonic bottle during the critical period when the poison would have been applied."

Moretti relaxed slightly, though suspicion lingered in his expression.

"And Mr Edwin Sykes," Mildred continued, glancing around the room though the critic was not present, "whose scathing reviews of Anton's performances established a public animosity between them, and whose hobby of butterfly collecting gave him access to cyanide. Yet his whereabouts throughout the evening are confirmed by multiple witnesses, placing him far from the backstage area during the crucial period when the poison must have been applied."

"Sylvia Harcourt," Mildred continued, turning toward the once-elegant patroness. "Your financial difficulties provided a compelling motive, particularly given your insurance policy on Anton's violin but not on his life. Anton's threats to expose your situation placed you in a desperate position."

Sylvia's solicitor leaned forward, ready to object, but she placed a restraining hand on his arm. "I have already admitted to planting evidence on Miss Bellamy," she said quietly. "But I did not kill Anton."

"Indeed," Mildred agreed. "Your actions after his death suggest opportunism rather than premeditation. You attempted to capitalise on a murder you did not commit, seeing a chance to divert suspicion and potentially benefit from the insurance claim when the violin later disappeared."

She turned her attention to Nora, who seemed to shrink under her gaze. "Nora Bellamy had reason to resent Anton after he withdrew her promised solo performance. A crushing disappointment for a young artist hoping for her breakthrough moment. Yet opportunity, again, was lacking. Multiple witnesses confirm you were practising in the musicians' common area during the critical period before the concert."

Nora's relief was palpable, her shoulders sagging as tears gathered in her eyes.

"Miss Winters," Mildred continued, glancing toward Lady Ivy's secretary. "Your connections to diplomatic circles that facilitated the violin's removal from the country are noted. The footprint at Volkov's was made by a heel still chipped; yours was already repaired. If you figure in this at all, it is as a facilitator of movements after the fact—not as the hand that ransacked, nor the hand that killed."

Miss Winters maintained her professional composure, though her hands clasped tightly before her.

Mildred paused, her gaze moving deliberately around the circle of suspects. The tension in the room had become almost tangible, every breath and movement magnified in the expectant silence.

"The method of murder," she resumed, "required not just opportunity, but intimate knowledge. Someone who understood precisely when and how Anton would uncork his tonic. Someone who had access to potassium cyanide and the expertise to apply it to the cork in a way that would activate only at the critical moment. Someone who stood to lose everything if Anton ended the arrangements that had been so profitable for all involved."

She lifted a final document from her portfolio. "Financial records obtained through Inspector Kent's connections reveal substantial debts owed to certain individuals connected with black market operations. Debts that were mysteriously cancelled the week after Anton's death."

Mildred surveyed the room once more, noting the subtle shifts in posture, the flickers of expression that betrayed inner turmoil. Moretti's scowl had deepened, though uncertainty now shadowed his eyes. Sylvia watched with wary attention, her fingers twisting her handkerchief. Nora seemed to breathe more freely, though she still darted nervous glances toward the door. Miss Winters remained outwardly composed, but her stillness had taken on a quality of alertness, like a bird poised for flight.

Only Otto Klein maintained his remarkable composure, his gaze steady, his hands relaxed in his lap. Yet something had changed in his eyes—a sharpening of focus, a heightened attention to Mildred's every word and movement.

"The evidence before us," Mildred said, her voice softening slightly, "points to someone who was present throughout Anton's career. Someone who travelled with him, who understood his habits and vulnerabilities. Someone who prepared his tonic before each performance, knowing he would uncork it himself precisely five minutes before stepping on stage."

She turned, finally, to face Otto directly. "Mr Klein. You had the most intimate knowledge of Anton's routines, having accompanied him for over fifteen years. You regularly prepared his tonic, though witnesses confirm Anton always uncorked it himself."

Otto met her gaze, the faintest flicker of something—annoyance, perhaps, or fear—passing across his features.

Mildred pressed on, her tone growing sharper. "And yet on the night of the concert, you were seen—alone—with Anton's case for several crucial minutes, breaking the routine even you yourself helped establish. Why, Mr Klein?"

The room waited, expectant. Otto's fingers twitched against the armrest. "There was nothing unusual. I was tuning—"

Bea spoke, voice trembling: "But Otto, didn't Mr Bishop say you wiped the mouth of the bottle? Why would you do that if you weren't…?"

Otto's mouth tightened, but he remained silent.

Mildred set down her next card: "A container of cyanide, disguised as rosin, was found in your office. Your sudden journey to Paris coincided exactly with the disappearance of the violin and a diplomatic courier crossing the Channel."

Mildred stepped toward him, voice low but clear. "You were desperate, weren't you? Debts, threats. But Anton was never merciful with debtors or rivals."

Still, Otto only stared at her coldly.

Now Mildred turned to the others, drawing them in:

"We've all wondered—why would someone so calm do something so monstrous? Because he was calm. Because he understood, better than anyone, the cost of not acting."

Silence. Heartbeats. Even Inspector Kent, usually controlled, seemed unable to breathe.

Sylvia whispered: "Otto, did you…?"

And then, finally, with a visible shudder, Otto broke his composure. He rose—not in calm resignation but with trembling hands, his voice at first barely above a whisper.

"I didn't want to. I prayed someone else would save him—from himself, from me. But Anton... would have destroyed us all. I was cornered—and yes, Lady Mildred, I was the only one close enough, invisible enough, to turn his rituals into his murderer."

Beats passed. Chairs scraped. Someone sobbed.

Otto's voice, steadying: "You want the method? Simple. After he left rehearsal, I used his own knife to lift the cork, painted the underside with cyanide, and pressed it back. I wiped away any trace with the same cloth he used to polish his violin. He trusted me. Until the end."

The assembled suspects stared. Even Mildred, trained to anticipate evil, felt the shock ripple through her chest.

"You all hid behind Anton's shadow," Otto spat, pain cracking the surface. "But in shadows, desperate men do what must be done."

Inspector Kent stood. The only sound was the tick of Lady Ivy's mantel clock.

As Kent prepared to escort Otto from the drawing room, the accompanist paused beside Mildred. "You were right about the cork," he said quietly. "A simple, elegant solution. Anton always appreciated elegance, even when he failed to embody it himself."

The admission, so casually delivered, sent a chill through the room. Lady Ivy gasped audibly, while Sylvia pressed a handkerchief to her lips. Moretti crossed himself, a reflexive gesture at odds with his usual cynicism.

As Kent led Otto away, the drawing room erupted into shocked murmurs. Bea moved to Mildred's side. "Well done," she murmured. "Though I must say, I never imagined quiet Otto capable of such calculation."

"Perhaps that was his greatest advantage," Mildred replied. "The ability to remain in the background, overlooked and underestimated, while orchestrating events with precision."

The case seemed resolved, the murderer identified and in custody. Yet something about Otto's parting words lingered in Mildred's mind, suggesting complexities yet to be fully understood. He had admitted to the murder, yes, but his reference to "certain parties" hinted at a wider conspiracy that remained partially obscured.

As the gathering dispersed, Mildred collected her evidence with methodical care. Otto Klein had acted as both accompanist and executioner to Anton Lanyi, but she sensed he was still, in some respects, merely following someone else's composition. The diplomatic connection that had facilitated the violin's removal from the country, the mysterious Miss Winters and her repaired heel, the powerful figures whose names had appeared in the smuggling ledger—all suggested a web of influence extending far beyond a single musician's revenge.

The final notes of this deadly symphony had yet to be played. And as she prepared to leave Lady Ivy's drawing room, Mildred wondered whose hand truly controlled the tempo of events that had led to Anton's final performance.

26

The morning following Otto Klein's dramatic confession brought a crisp autumn day, the kind that seemed to mock the gravity of recent events with its brilliant sunshine and cloudless sky. Mildred sat in her study, arranging the scattered remnants of the investigation into orderly piles. Otto was now in custody, charged with Anton Lanyi's murder, but numerous loose threads remained to be gathered and understood.

A light tap at the door announced Perkins. "Inspector Kent to see you, my lady. He says it's a matter of some importance."

Kent entered with less formality than usual, his demeanour suggesting both triumph and lingering questions. "Good morning, Lady Mildred. I thought you might appreciate an update on certain developments."

"Please," she gestured to the chair opposite her desk. "I assume there's been progress with Otto?"

"He's made a full confession," Kent confirmed, settling into the chair. "Remarkably detailed, in fact. He describes applying the cyanide to the cork with meticulous precision, knowing Anton would uncork the bottle himself at exactly five minutes before performance. For the record, we aren't relying on that rosin box from his office; the room wasn't sealed when it was first found and the item adds little against the cork analysis and his own account."

"A chillingly calculated method," Mildred observed. "Has he revealed his motive beyond what we already surmised?"

"Financial desperation, primarily. He owed substantial sums to certain individuals who were growing impatient. When Anton threatened to end their smuggling arrangements, Otto faced complete ruin." Kent hesitated, then added, "But there's a broader context emerging. Otto wasn't working alone in the smuggling operations, merely in the murder itself."

"I suspected as much," Mildred said. "The diplomatic connection that facilitated the violin's removal from the country suggested a web of influence extending beyond a single musician's revenge."

"Indeed. And that brings me to the purpose of my visit." Kent leaned forward, his professional demeanour softening slightly. "Arthur Pike has come forward with information about the violin's disappearance."

"Pike?" Mildred's eyebrows rose in surprise. "I thought he'd been cleared of involvement."

"In the murder, yes. But it seems he played a role in the subsequent theft of the violin from police custody." Kent consulted his notebook. "He arrived at the Yard this morning, quite agitated, insisting on making a statement. According to Pike, he was approached by two men claiming to represent Sir Basil Thornton."

"Sir Basil?" The name was familiar to Mildred—a wealthy industrialist with significant diplomatic connections, particularly in Eastern Europe. "What would he want with Anton's violin?"

"Not the violin itself, but what it contained," Kent explained. "According to Pike, these men made it clear that certain documents hidden within the instrument needed to be retrieved before they fell into the 'wrong hands.' They offered him a substantial sum, coupled with thinly veiled threats about his gambling debts."

"So Pike arranged the violin's removal using his knowledge of the building's service passages," Mildred concluded. "The laundry chute we discovered."

"Precisely. He claims he was merely the facilitator, providing access and information but not handling the violin himself. That task fell to a woman matching Miss Winters' description, though Pike knew her only as 'the secretary.'"

Mildred considered this revelation, mentally connecting it to the footprint with the chipped heel found in Volkov's ransacked workshop. "And has Sir Basil been questioned?"

"That's where matters become complicated," Kent admitted with evident frustration. "Sir Basil is currently serving as a trade envoy in Prague, and his diplomatic status makes formal interrogation difficult. When approached by our colleagues at the Foreign Office, he expressed shock and denied any knowledge of the affair, suggesting his name had been used without authorisation."

"A convenient position," Mildred observed dryly.

"Indeed. Though proving otherwise may prove impossible, given the channels through which these operations were conducted." Kent's expression suggested this outcome particularly galled him. "In any case, Pike has been charged with obstruction and theft, though he maintains he never intended harm to anyone and knew nothing of Anton's murder beforehand."

"I'm inclined to believe him on that point," Mildred said. "His panic when we discovered the laundry chute seemed genuine, and Otto's confession makes no mention of Pike as an accomplice in the murder."

Kent nodded, then shifted to another topic. "As for Mrs Harcourt, I'm afraid her situation has deteriorated considerably."

"How so?"

"Her insurance claim on the violin has been formally denied, and Lloyd's is investigating potential fraud. More damaging still, her admission to planting evidence on Miss Bellamy has become public knowledge. She's been essentially ostracised from society, though she may avoid prison by cooperating with our investigation into the wider smuggling network."

Mildred felt a complex mixture of sympathy and disapproval for Sylvia. The woman's actions had been born of desperation rather than malice, yet they had nearly sent an innocent young woman to the gallows. "And what of Nora? Has she been formally cleared?"

"Yes, with apologies from the Yard," Kent replied, a hint of genuine regret in his tone. "Though I fear the damage to her reputation may prove lasting. The public remembers accusations more vividly than retractions."

"Perhaps," Mildred agreed. "But youth and talent have remarkable resilience. With proper support, she may yet recover her standing."

"Speaking of resilience," Kent continued, "Maestro Moretti has been surprisingly magnanimous since Otto's confession. He's arranged a memorial concert for Anton, with proceeds to benefit young musicians from Central Europe. Quite a transformation from his earlier vitriol."

"Grief and suspicion affect people in strange ways," Mildred observed. "Moretti's temper made him an obvious suspect, which likely intensified his defensiveness. With that cloud lifted, his better nature has space to emerge."

"And let's not forget Sykes," Kent said as he scratched the stubble on his face. "He's published a surprisingly sympathetic obituary of Anton. Perhaps guilt over their public feuding, or simply recognition that a virtuoso's death sells more papers than a critic's spite."

Their conversation was interrupted by Bea's arrival, announced by her distinctive rapid knock before Perkins could properly announce her. She swept in, elegantly attired despite the early hour, her expression animated with fresh gossip.

"Mildred, darling, you won't believe what I've just heard! Oh, Inspector Kent, how splendid to find you here. You've saved me the trouble of telephoning the Yard."

"Good morning, Lady Beatrice," Kent replied with the resigned patience of one accustomed to her dramatic entrances. "What news brings you here in such haste?"

"Sir Basil Thornton's secretary has resigned!" Bea announced, settling herself on the sofa. "Left without notice, apparently. My cousin Georgina's husband works at the Foreign Office, and he says the poor man is absolutely frantic, searching for some missing diplomatic pouch. The timing seems rather significant, wouldn't you agree?"

Kent and Mildred exchanged a look of shared understanding. "This secretary," Kent asked carefully. "Would her name happen to be Margaret Winters?"

"The very same!" Bea confirmed triumphantly. "Quite an efficient woman by all accounts, though rather cold. Georgina met her at some dreary diplomatic function last year and found her utterly forgettable until this sudden disappearance."

"Miss Winters," Mildred mused. "Lady Ivy's secretary with the repaired heel, and now, it seems, Sir Basil's as well. How interesting that she managed to occupy both positions simultaneously."

"A convenient arrangement for maintaining surveillance on musical circles while serving diplomatic interests," Kent observed. "Though I suspect she's well beyond our reach by now, probably on the Continent with a new identity."

The three sat in thoughtful silence for a moment, each contemplating the expanding web of intrigue that had begun with a violinist's collapse and now stretched across international borders.

Bea was the first to break the silence. "Well, I think we deserve tea after all these revelations. Perkins mentioned there are fresh scones."

As they moved to the drawing room for refreshments, the conversation shifted to the aftermath of Otto's arrest. Nora had returned to her lodgings, shaken but relieved by her exoneration. Moretti had thrown himself into preparations for the memorial concert, perhaps finding redemption through music. Sylvia Harcourt had retreated to her country estate, her London townhouse already listed for sale.

"It's remarkable how quickly life reorganises itself after such disruption," Mildred observed as Perkins served the tea. "Each person adjusting to their new reality, for better or worse."

"Though not all threads are so neatly tied," Kent reminded her. "Sir Basil remains untouchable, Miss Winters has vanished, and whatever documents were hidden in Anton's violin are now beyond our reach."

"True," Mildred acknowledged. "But Otto will face justice for Anton's murder, Nora has been cleared of false accusations, and the wider smuggling operation has been exposed, even if some participants escape consequences."

"Speaking of consequences," Bea interjected, stirring an excessive amount of sugar into her tea, "have you heard what's happened to Volkov? His workshop has been positively inundated with customers since the news broke. Apparently, notoriety is good for business in certain circles."

Kent frowned. "I'm not sure I approve of him profiting from his connection to this case. He did, after all, construct the hidden compartments that facilitated the smuggling."

"Under duress, by his account," Mildred reminded him. "And he's paid a price in his own way. His workshop was ransacked, his safety threatened. Perhaps this unexpected prosperity is a form of karmic balance."

"You're becoming philosophical in your victory, Lady Mildred," Kent observed with a slight smile. "Though I wouldn't characterise this case as fully resolved. Too many questions remain unanswered."

"True resolution is rare in human affairs," she replied. "We've uncovered the truth about Anton's death, which was our primary objective. The wider implications of his smuggling activities may never be fully mapped, particularly given the diplomatic complications."

As their discussion continued, Mildred found herself reflecting on the complex moral landscape the case had revealed. Otto

Klein, the quiet accompanist who had poisoned his longtime musical partner out of financial desperation. Sylvia Harcourt, the elegant patroness driven to frame an innocent girl to protect her crumbling social position. Arthur Pike, the pragmatic stage manager, was coerced into facilitating theft through a combination of bribery and threats. Each had made choices born of fear, ambition, or survival instinct, with consequences that rippled outward to touch countless lives.

Even now, with the central mystery solved, those ripples continued to spread. Nora would carry the shadow of her false arrest for years to come, despite her formal exoneration. Moretti might find a measure of redemption through his memorial concert, or he might slip back into bitterness once the spotlight faded. Sylvia faced social ruin, her carefully maintained façade of prosperity finally shattered beyond repair.

"As for Sir Basil and Miss Winters," Kent said, "her movements align with facilitation after the theft, not with the break--in or the murder; beyond that, diplomacy muddies more than it clears."

The afternoon was drawing to a close when Kent finally took his leave, pausing at the door to offer a rare compliment. "Your insights were invaluable in this case, Lady Mildred. Particularly regarding the poisoned cork. Without that discovery, we might never have identified the true method or killer."

"Thank you, Inspector," she replied, genuinely appreciative of his acknowledgment. "Though I suspect our collaboration may have been more successful had you been less resistant to my involvement initially."

Kent's expression suggested grudging agreement. "Perhaps next time, I'll be more receptive to your observations from the outset."

"Next time?" Mildred raised an eyebrow. "I rather hope there won't be another murder requiring our combined efforts."

"As do I," Kent conceded. "But London is a city of secrets, Lady Mildred. I wouldn't be surprised if our paths cross professionally again."

After his departure, Bea lingered, helping Mildred organise the last of her case notes. "It's all rather sad, isn't it?" she remarked, uncharacteristically subdued. "Otto seemed so devoted to Anton. To think he was planning his death while preparing his tonic, standing beside him at countless performances."

"The closest relationships often contain the deepest capacity for betrayal," Mildred replied. "Otto knew Anton better than anyone—his habits, his vulnerabilities, his secrets. That intimacy gave him both motive and opportunity."

As the evening shadows lengthened across her study, Mildred found herself returning to the annotated sheet music that had first captured her attention. The coded markings, some genuine and others falsified, told a story of smuggling, secrecy, and ultimately murder. Yet even these tangible pieces of evidence couldn't fully explain the human complexities behind them—the fears, ambitions, and compromises that had led to Anton Lanyi's final performance.

Tomorrow would bring new developments: Pike's formal statement, perhaps further revelations about Sir Basil's involvement, preparations for Otto's trial. The ripples would continue to spread, touching lives far removed from the Royal Albert Hall where Anton had collapsed. And somewhere in Europe, a woman with a recently repaired heel was disappearing into the shadows, carrying secrets that might never come to light.

The case was solved, yet not truly concluded. And as Mildred carefully filed away the last of her notes, she couldn't help wondering what other threads remained hidden, waiting to be discovered by those patient enough to follow where they led.

———

As the evening shadows lengthened across her study, Mildred closed her case journal with a sense of finality. Three weeks after Otto's confession, the world had largely moved on. Moretti's memorial concert had briefly rekindled public interest in Anton's legacy, though focused now on his artistry rather than his death. Nora had accepted a position with a provincial orchestra, where her talent might flourish away from London's memories. Sylvia had retreated to Bath, where judgments were softer and the waters promised healing. Even Kent had returned to his normal duties, though their parting had held a warmth that surprised them both.

Mildred gazed out at her garden, now settling into autumn dormancy. The urgency of investigation had given way to quiet reflection, and she found herself looking forward to simpler pleasures: Henry's chess matches by the fire, Bea's theatrical visits, perhaps even a winter holiday in the countryside. Yet as she placed Anton's annotated music into her desk drawer, she couldn't help but smile at herself. Peace and tranquillity would be welcome, certainly—but her mind, once trained to see patterns and secrets, would never truly rest. London would always harbour its mysteries, hidden behind drawing room curtains or whispered in theatre corridors. For now, though, she was content to let them find someone else.

The teacup at her elbow had grown cold; she would have Perkins bring a fresh pot. Perhaps with those currant scones

Henry so enjoyed. The simple pleasures, after all, were what made the darker mysteries of human nature bearable. And should another puzzle eventually find its way to her door—well, that was tomorrow's concern.

The End

AFTERWORD

Thank you for reading *The Mystery of the Vanishing Violinist*. I really hope you enjoyed reading it as much as I had writing it!

If you have a minute, please consider leaving a review on Amazon or the retailer where you got it.

Many thanks in advance for your support!

THE MYSTERY OF THE CHRISTMAS MINCE PIES

CHAPTER 1 SNEAK PEEK

Lady Mildred Ramsay sat at her writing desk, silver letter opener poised above the cream envelope that had arrived with the morning post. The Mayfair Club's distinctive crest was impressed in scarlet wax—a stylised "M" encircled by holly leaves. She examined it with the careful attention she once gave to bandages and morphine doses during the war, noting the slight unevenness in the seal's impression that suggested haste.

The gentle warmth of the drawing room fire did little to dispel the December chill that had settled over London like a damp woollen blanket. Outside, frost gilded the windowpanes, transforming the garden into a silvery wonderland that shimmered in the late morning light. From somewhere in the house came the distant hum of a Christmas carol being hummed by the maid.

"For heaven's sake, Millie, just open it," said Lady Beatrice Mortimer from her perch on the window seat. "Your scrutiny won't reveal its contents any faster than actually reading it."

Mildred's lips quirked into a half-smile. "A nurse's habit, Bea. Observation before action."

"Well, observe a bit faster. I'm positively perishing with curiosity."

With a precise flick of her wrist, Mildred sliced the envelope open and extracted a heavy card embossed with gold. Her dark eyes scanned the elegant script, noting the flourishes that adorned each letter, the calligrapher had been well paid for their services.

"The Mayfair Club requests the pleasure of my company at their annual Christmas charity fête," she read aloud. "December twenty-first, seven o'clock. Evening dress. Donations for war widows and orphans graciously accepted."

"Oh, how perfectly splendid!" Bea exclaimed, abandoning her post by the window to peer over Mildred's shoulder. "I received mine yesterday and have already sent my acceptance. We shall have such fun, and just imagine the gossip—Lady Ivy's new turban alone will be worth the price of admission."

Mildred set the invitation on her desk with deliberate care. "I hadn't planned on attending."

"Nonsense," came a voice from the doorway. Lord Henry Ramsay stood there, newspaper tucked under his arm, the very picture of aristocratic propriety in his tweed suit and perfectly polished shoes. "Of course you'll attend. The Mayfair Club's Christmas fête is the social event of the season."

"Which is precisely why I had planned to avoid it," Mildred replied dryly. "An evening of insincere pleasantries and competitive philanthropy holds limited appeal."

Henry sighed, entering the room with the resigned air of an older brother accustomed to his sister's recalcitrance. "It's not merely about social obligations, Millie. It's about being seen doing good. The charity benefits war widows—a cause I would have thought you'd support, given your nursing service."

Mildred felt the familiar pang that always accompanied mentions of the war. Four years in field hospitals had left her with more than just memories; it had fundamentally altered how she viewed the polite fictions of society. "I support the cause, Henry. I simply question whether it requires my physical presence amid London's most determined social climbers."

"Oh, don't be such a wet blanket," Bea chided, dropping gracefully onto the settee and arranging her skirts with artful casualness. "Christmas comes but once a year, and after all those dreary months at Highfield Manor and that frightful business at Brooklands, we deserve a little festive cheer."

"Murder investigations are hardly 'dreary,' Bea," Mildred pointed out.

"Well, no, they're positively thrilling. But one can't spend all one's time solving mysteries. Besides," she added with a conspiratorial gleam in her eye, "Inspector Kent is rumoured to be attending. In an official capacity, of course."

Mildred ignored the knowing look her friend sent her way. Her occasional collaborations with Detective Inspector Charles Kent were a subject Bea found endlessly fascinating and frequently misinterpreted.

"The Mayfair Club's mince pies are legendary," Bea continued, changing tactics. "Mrs Penworthy guards the recipe like crown jewels, and Chef Duval's brandy butter is positively sinful. It shall be a feast of mince pies and mischief, mark my words."

Henry seized on this more practical argument. "There you are, then. Excellent food, a worthy cause, and a respectable gathering. I'm sure Father would expect our family to be represented."

Mildred suppressed a sigh. The invocation of their father's expectations was Henry's trump card, and they all knew it. She glanced down at the invitation again, tracing the embossed lettering with her fingertip. Perhaps Bea was right—after the intensity of her recent investigations, an evening of trivial socialising might provide a welcome change of pace. And the cause was undeniably worthy.

"Very well," she conceded, her tone suggesting a greater sacrifice than was actually being made. "I shall attend this festival of forced goodwill and competitive charity."

"Splendid!" Bea clapped her hands in delight. "I've already had Simmons begin pressing your emerald evening gown. It brings out the green flecks in your eyes."

"Of course you have," Mildred said with resigned affection. Bea's presumptuous certainty that she would eventually agree was both irritating and endearing. "Is there anything else you've arranged without my knowledge?"

"Only a hair appointment on the morning of the event," Bea replied cheerfully. "And I may have mentioned to Lady Ivy that you'd be delighted to judge the Christmas pudding competition."

Henry cleared his throat to disguise what sounded suspiciously like a chuckle. "I'll have Thompson bring the Daimler round at half-past six. Best to arrive fashionably late, but not rudely so."

As her brother departed to attend to his correspondence, Mildred turned back to the window. The London sky was heavy with the promise of snow, grey clouds hanging low over the chimney pots and spires. She had a sudden, inexplicable feeling that this Christmas season would bring more than just the usual round of festivities and social obligations.

"A penny for your thoughts," Bea said, coming to stand beside her.

Mildred smiled faintly. "I was just thinking that Christmas at the Mayfair Club should be relatively uncomplicated. No disappearing diamonds or racing car sabotage to contend with."

"Just mince pies, carols, and charitable giving," Bea agreed. "Though with Mrs Penworthy presiding over proceedings, there's bound to be some drama. The woman collects grudges like others collect porcelain figurines."

"Well, let us hope any drama remains firmly in the realm of social faux pas rather than felony," Mildred replied, slipping the invitation into her desk drawer. "I've had quite enough of crime for one year."

Bea's laughter filled the room like champagne bubbles. "Oh, Millie. You know perfectly well that trouble finds you whether you seek it or not. It's part of your charm."

As the first snowflakes began to drift past the window, Mildred allowed herself a small smile. Perhaps Bea was right —perhaps a bit of festive frivolity was exactly what she needed. And if the evening proved dull, she could always entertain herself by observing the secret dramas playing out beneath the glittering surface of London society.

After all, people were always more interesting than they appeared at first glance. It was a lesson she had learned well, both as a nurse and as an accidental detective. Behind every polite smile lay a story—sometimes charming, sometimes tragic, and occasionally deadly.

But surely not at the Mayfair Club's Christmas charity fête. This year, for once, she would simply enjoy the season without mystery or mayhem intruding.

Or so she hoped.

Get your copy at all good retailers.

ALSO BY RUTH BAKER

The Ivy Creek Cozy Mystery Series

Which Pie Goes with Murder? (Book 1)
Twinkle, Twinkle, Deadly Sprinkles (Book 2)
Eat Once, Die Twice (Book 3)
Silent Night, Unholy Bites (Book 4)
Waffles and Scuffles (Book 5)
Cookie Dough and Bruised Egos (Book 6)
A Sticky Toffee Catastrophe (Book 7)
Dough Shall Not Murder (Book 8)
Deadly Bites on Winter Nights (Book 9)
A Juicy Steak Tragedy (Book 10)
Southern Fried and Grief Stricken (Book 11)
Poisoned Freebies at Phoebe's (Book 12)
Tasty Edibles, Nasty Rumblings (Book 13)
A Spicy Side of Homicide (Book 14)
The Wedding Cake Conundrum (Book 15)

The Whispering Haven Cozy Mystery Series

Gone in a Snap (Book 1)
Say Cheese and Die Laughing (Book 2)
Deadly Flash from the Past (Book 3)
Framed in Mischief (Book 4)
Silent Night, Deadly Light (Book 5)
Focal Point Fiasco (Book 6)

The Lady Mildred Ramsay Murder Mystery Series

The Mystery of the Disappearing Diamonds (Book 1)
The Mystery of the Final Lap (Book 2)
The Mystery of the Vanishing Violinist (Book 3)
The Mystery of the Christmas Mince Pies (Book 4)

NEWSLETTER SIGNUP

Want **FREE** COPIES OF FUTURE **CLEANTALES** BOOKS, FIRST NOTIFICATION OF NEW RELEASES, CONTESTS AND GIVEAWAYS?

GO TO THE LINK BELOW TO SIGN UP TO THE NEWSLETTER!

https://cleantales.com/newsletter/

Printed in Dunstable, United Kingdom